PRAISE FOR STEPHEN LEATHER

'A writer at the top of his game'
Sunday Express

'A master of the thriller genre'
Irish Times

'Let Spider draw you into his web, you won't regret it'
The Sun

'The sheer impetus of his storytelling is damned hard to resist'
Daily Express

'High-adrenaline plotting'
Sunday Express

'Written with panache, and a fine ear for dialogue, Leather manages the collision between the real and the occult with exceptional skill, adding a superb time-shift twist at the end'
Daily Mail on *Nightmare*

'A wicked read'
Anthony Horowitz on *Nightfall*

'In brisk newman's style he explores complex contemporary issues while keeping the action fast and bloody'
Economist

'Stephen Leather is one of our most prolific and successful crime writers ... A disturbing, blood-chilling read from a writer at the top of his game'
Sunday Express on *Midnight*

'Lots of gunfire, tactical talk and imaginative plotting. Let Spider draw you into his web, you won't regret it'
The Sun on the *Spider Shepherd thrillers*

'He has the uncanny knack of producing plots that are all too real, and this is no exception. It is the authenticity of this plot that grasps the imagination and never lets it go'
Daily Mail on *First Response*

Plausible Deniability

Also by Stephen Leather

Pay Off
The Fireman
Hungry Ghost
The Chinaman
The Vets
The Long Shot
The Birthday Girl
The Double Tap
The Solitary Man
The Tunnel Rats
The Bombmaker
The Stretch
Tango One
The Eyewitness
Penalties
Takedown
The Shout
The Bag Carrier

Spider Shepherd thrillers:
Hard Landing
Soft Target
Cold Kill
Hot Blood
Dead Men
Live Fire
Rough Justice
Fair Game
False Friends
True Colours
White Lies
Black Ops
Dark Forces
Light Touch
Tall Order
Short Range

Spider Shepherd: SAS thrillers :
The Sandpit
Moving Targets

Jack Nightingale supernatural thrillers:
Nightfall
Midnight
Nightmare
Nightshade
Lastnight
San Francisco Night
New York Night
Tennessee Night

Plausible Deniability

Stephen Leather

Chapter 1

Dawn was still streaking the eastern sky when a figure emerged from one of the apartment buildings fronting Pattaya Beach. Lex Harper crossed the road to the walkway along the edge of the beach, took a few deep breaths and then began to run. He settled at once into a steady pace, his long stride eating up the metres. The air was as close to cool as it ever was in Pattaya and this early in the morning, the walkway was still virtually deserted. A few drunken tourists were sleeping it off under the palm trees, some of whom would wake to find that their wallets had been stolen by the thieves and pickpockets that prowled the beaches during the night looking for victims. However, most of the tourists were still in bed and the stall-holders, street vendors, prostitutes, lady-boys and the rest of the multitude of traders and petty criminals who operated on the strip, pandering to the tourists or preying on them, had yet to begin business for the day.

As usual, Harper ran the three miles to the city's main entertainment area, Walking Street, where among the town's raunchier go-go bars almost any sexual taste and preference could be catered for - at a price. At night it was a neon-lit maelstrom of sex tourists, tour groups, hookers, lady-boys and loud-mouthed touts shouting the delights of bars, sex shows and clip joints. Daylight revealed it as a shabby ghost town, with potholed roads and pavements, fly-blown shopfronts with peeling paint, and neon signs connected to electrical wiring that would have been banned as unsafe in any country in the First World.

He drank a bottle of water and then ran back along the beach, sprinting the last mile flat out. He showered and dressed, then took a cup of coffee out onto the wraparound balcony of his three-bed penthouse apartment, with spectacular views out over the bay. He was just finishing the last mouthful of coffee when he felt a vibration from the denim hip pack around his waist. He always had the hip pack on him, no matter what the time of day. It contained one of his many phones, an Irish passport in a false name, two credit cards under the same name and fifty-thousand baht - just over £1,100 - in cash. The pack and the heavy gold neck chain he always wore, meant that he could always leave the country at a moment's notice, either through the airport or overland to Laos, Cambodia, Malaysia or even Myanmar and live a below-the-radar existence for as long as was necessary to avoid or eliminate the threat to him. He had a larger bug-out bag under the emperor-size bed in his apartment and another in a specially constructed compartment under the floor of his SUV, but the essentials were in the hip pack. He loved Thailand, the Land Of Smiles, but if necessary, his unbreakable, life-preserving rule was always to be ready to leave any place, at a moment's notice, without ever looking back.

The text message was from a number he didn't recognise and said only 'YOU HAVE MAIL', but Harper smiled, finished his coffee and then headed back into the streets to a combination internet café and beauty parlour a little way along the beach road. There were only three other customers, a middle-aged European man hunched over one of the terminals, planning his day's itinerary or watching a little breakfast porn, and a couple of bar-girls, one having her nails done and the other browsing the internet before starting her shift. The owner of the shop, Khun Bee, was in her late fifties with greying hair and deep lines on her face, but she still had the body of a much younger woman, in tribute to the years she had spent earning her living pole-dancing at a bar a few metres further up the street. She greeted Harper with a smile, took the money he gave her for half an hour's internet use and waved a hand in the direction of the terminals. 'Any you like, Lek.' Most Thais had a problem pronouncing Lex and Lek was a common nickname in Thailand. It meant small, and Harper had long ago accepted it as his Thai name.

He took the terminal furthest away from the counter, tilted the screen to hide it from the other customers and logged on. He knew the email address and password as well as he knew his own name, even though the account had never been used to send a single email. Its only purpose was to allow for secure communications between him and his handler, Charlotte Button, formerly of MI5 but now controlling a shadowy, strictly deniable organisation that handled jobs that were too risky, too politically sensitive or too illegal for government spooks to touch. It was known to those who worked for it as The Pool, partly because of the fluid nature of the group but also because a substantial number of its members, like Harper, came from Liverpool.

The Pool was a commercial organisation, largely funded by the UK government but run at arm's length from it. Most of the company's business was legitimate: bodyguarding, training the security personnel of Western allies and client states, supervising the security of buildings, plants and installations in sensitive areas. They even had a maritime division combating piracy around the Gulf and the Horn of Africa. All these activities and other, even more clandestine ones, would once have been carried out by British troops, British spooks or British government agencies, but in common with the US, in a policy described as "Secure Outsourcing", more and more secret operations were now kept off the books and contracted out to private companies.

The source of much of the company's very substantial budget was still primarily Her Majesty's

Government, but the money was paid through offshore accounts several times removed from the true source allowing the government and its agencies to deny all knowledge of it and responsibility for it. If anything ever went wrong, it was the company, not the UK government that had to take the flak.

Button and Harper were the only people who could access the email account and they used the Draft folder to send messages to each other, a technique borrowed from al-Qaeda terrorists who had developed it to communicate without being detected by even the most high-tech surveillance systems. If an email had ever actually been sent, it could have been intercepted and read by operatives at the National Security Agency in the US and GCHQ in the UK, who had the capacity to eavesdrop on any phone call and intercept any email anywhere in the world. However, since no emails were ever transmitted from the account, its existence and its content remained unknown to all but the two people who used it. Only if a spook had discovered its existence and hacked into it, would messages in the Drafts folder be compromised, but even then, it would have to have been monitored constantly, since their SOP was to delete every message as soon as it had been read.

Harper found a message summoning him to a meeting with Button in Bangkok later that afternoon, which surprised him because so far as he was aware, Button rarely left the UK.

He jogged back to his apartment, showered and changed into a polo shirt and jeans, then headed down to a British restaurant where he had a full English – eggs, bacon, sausage, black pudding, baked beans, mushrooms and fried bread and two more cups of coffee.

He drove the 150 kilometres to Bangkok in just over two hours. Button was staying at the JW Marriott in Sukhumvit Road, one of the city's best hotels. It was a short walk from the Nana Plaza red light area, but Harper was sure that Button wouldn't be dropping by. He parked in the hotel's car park. Button had given him the room number and the name she was staying under, so he bypassed reception and went straight up.

He knocked on the door and she made him wait almost a minute before opening it, which he assumed was her way of asserting dominance. But when the door finally opened she was holding her mobile and she flashed him an apologetic smile and waved him in.

She was in a suite and from the look of it she had only just arrived. Her Louis Vuitton suitcase was on a stand by the door, unopened and the bed hadn't been disturbed. She was wearing one of her signature Chanel suits and her chestnut hair was shorter than last time he'd seen her. She smiled again and pointed at the minibar and Harper helped himself to a water while she finished her call.

'Sorry about that, Lex,' she said. 'It's a flying visit so I've a lot to pack in.'

'I'm just pleased that the mountain has come to Mohammed for once,' he said, sitting down on the bed. 'Usually I have to fly half way across the world for a meeting.'

'We're about to do some work for the Thai Government and there are some i's to be dotted and t's to be crossed.'

'Getting into bed with a military dictatorship is never a good idea,' said Harper. He took a sip of water.

'The Thais are having trouble with Muslim militants in the South and have requested our expertise,' she said. 'I haven't mentioned it to you because it's never a good idea to shit on your own doorstep.'

He raised his water bottle in salute. 'Much appreciated,' he said.

'Anyway, enough chit chat,' she said. Sitting down at a teak desk and demurely crossing her legs. There was a slim leather briefcase on the desk and she snapped open the locks and pulled out a file. 'A decision has now been taken at the very highest level to change the focus on the war on drugs. The US President has got tired of waiting for results he can crow about from Central America, so he has taken the unilateral decision to switch the attack to the heroin fields in the Myanmar part of the Golden Triangle.'

Harper gave a sour smile. 'Nothing beats the quick fix for a politician, does it? Especially in an election year. And presumably our own PM has fallen into line as usual.'

'Correct.'

'And equally, the President will not be wanting to risk any US personnel on the mission, in case it all goes to ratshit.'

'As you say. So the mission is to eliminate the whole of this year's heroin crop before it can be processed and transported to the US, either by destroying it or by cutting a deal to buy it. I can give you carte blanche on methods and tactics, but as ever, and even more so in this case, it is a completely deniable mission. Once you're out there, you're on your own. If you're compromised, the UK and US governments and agencies will never even have heard of you.' She paused. 'However, the cousins are happy to throw money at this to get a result and that being so, the tidiest way to achieve the aim would probably just be to buy the whole crop and then, once we've secured it, the cousins can arrange its destruction at their leisure.'

'The Yanks are going to buy the crop? The whole crop?'

'That's the plan, yes.'

'How exactly? Paypal? Or one of those super big cheques you see on TV?'

'I'll come on to the specifics,' she said. 'The plan is for you to go in with a support team who will be supplied covertly by the authorities here: six ex-Thai special forces soldiers who have all been operating illicitly in the target area of southern Myanmar. The Thai special forces speak the local languages and have already had dealings with the drug lords.

They'll give you back up and protection, and lead you to the RV, deep inside Myanmar.'

'The Thai special forces are all trained by the Americans,' Harper said, 'so they won't be that special, will they?'

Button pursed her lips. 'Be that as it may, they speak the language, know the terrain and can get you face to face with the warlords who control heroin production there, so they should earn their keep.'

Harper included his head. 'Fair enough. And what will I be taking to these warlords?'

'Well, the days of making pay-offs in gold have long gone and in any case, it would take a truck to carry the amount of gold bullion we're talking about, so the idea is to make a payment of ten million dollars in bearer bonds.'

'Bearer bonds?' Harper said, 'are they even a thing anymore? I thought the Yanks had banned them a few years ago.'

'They did, because they were so widely used by money launderers, drug lords and tax evaders, but other countries still issue and cash them.'

Harper smiled. 'So the country that banned them is now making use of someone else's? I've said it before and I'll say it again, Americans have no sense of irony. Anyway, irrespective of how the cash is going to be paid, you won't buy the heroin crop for $10 million, it's got to be worth at least 100 times that amount.'

'Obviously,' Button said, sounding like a primary school teacher waiting for a rather slow-witted pupil to catch up. 'The $10 million is just a down payment to show good faith and get the attention of the warlords. A much larger sum will be paid to complete the deal.'

'The cousins better have deep pockets then,' Harper said, 'because I can't see the warlords listening to offers much below $1 billion.'

'Maybe so, but when you consider that the US Congress put the cost of US involvement in Iraq and Afghanistan at $2.5 trillion, a billion to shut down a substantial part of the world's heroin trade might seem like a bit of a bargain.' She paused. 'Anyway, that will only be payable on receipt of the crop, and by then your involvement should be over. If all has gone to plan, the cousins will be willing to put their own heads above the parapet.'

'Just in time for the photo-ops for US domestic consumption,' Harper said. 'I can see the headlines now. "POTUS's decisive action deals fatal blow to heroin trade." And there'll be a tiny bit of reflected glory for our own PM too - just a little, not too much.'

'Such cynicism, Lex,' Button said with mock severity.

'Anyway, it sounds like the deal's already been done,' Harper said. 'So why do you need me to be a very expensive delivery boy?'

'Because you're entering one of the most unpredictable and lawless areas on the planet and as I'm sure you know, bearer bonds are quite literally as good as gold. No proof of ownership is necessary or possible because possession of bearer bonds is not just nine points of the law; it's all ten. If you have them in your possession, you are the rightful owner, QED. So you're there to use any means necessary to keep those bonds out of unfriendly hands and deliver them safely to the drug lords, but only once you've satisfied yourself that they'll keep their end of the deal.'

'And if anything does go wrong, the Yanks don't want an American involved?'

'It gives the Americans plausible deniability, yes.'

'And you're trusting me not to just trouser the bonds myself and do a runner?'

She gave a smile in which her eyes played no part. 'You could do that, of course, but you would then spend the rest of your life looking over your shoulder and I can promise you that the duration of that life would be very short. You're not the only hired killer on my books, Lex.'

'I'm sure I'm not, Charlie, but I am the best. Anyway, don't get your expensive silk underwear in a twist, I'm not about to do a runner, I enjoy our relationship too much.' He grinned. 'And who knows, one day, it might be more than strictly business ...'

Button rolled her eyes. 'I'm not always sure exactly what my type is, Lex, but one thing I am sure of, whatever it is, you're not it.'

He burst out laughing and took another sip of water. They spent another hour discussing the finer details of the plan and studying the mapping and satellite imagery of the target area that Button had brought with her. 'That's what's driving the policy, isn't it?' Harper said. 'Suddenly everyone's an expert. The guys behind their desks at GCHQ and Northwood, and at the NSA, the DEA and the Pentagon in Washington, can call up an image from anywhere on the planet, and if they can see it, they think it must be easy to go in and solve the problem. But seeing it from a satellite and actually getting to it are two very different things.'

'Which is why we use people with skill-sets like yours.' She flashed him a tight smile.

'So what are you going to be doing while I'm risking life and limb, Charlie? Glyndebourne? Royal Ascot? Cowdray Park for the polo?'

'Believe it or not, Lex, I'm going to take a little holiday in Phuket.'

'A holiday? You? I didn't think you did things like that, least of all in a place like Phuket. Are you sure you're not just doing it to keep within range of me and those bearer bonds?'

She gave an enigmatic smile. 'Heavens no, Lex, you know I'd trust you with my life.'

'And the money?'

Her smile widened. 'Not so much.'

'And where are they, these bonds?'

Button stood up and walked over to the suitcase. She opened it and lifted the lid. Inside the case was a grey aluminium tube. She took it out and gave it to him. It weighed less than a kilo and he grinned at her. 'You'd have thought ten million dollars would be heavier,' he said.

Chapter 2

Harper booked himself into a hotel much less salubrious than the JW Marriott, then made some purchases from a warehouse in Bangkok that sold high end security and surveillance equipment. He bought an untraceable weapon and ammunition from a contact whose day job as a Thai army quartermaster gave him access to US-supplied weaponry, some of which he then sold on the black market. He left the bonds and the purchases in his SUV, then made his way downtown to Khlong Toei, the worst of the worst areas of the city, where he linked up with the ex-Thai special forces who were to be his escort in and out of Myanmar. There was a sergeant, Narong, a corporal, Decha, and four other soldiers. As Narong introduced the rest of his men, Harper said 'You speak very good English.'

Narong shrugged. 'We were trained by the Americans and - like you British - they speak no language but their own and expect everyone else to learn theirs.'

Harper inclined his head in acknowledgment of that. Narong's men, all tattooed and unshaven, had an arrogance about them that Harper found disquieting and as soon as he met them he had misgivings about using them because they appeared to be operating right on the edge. They were undisciplined by special forces' standards and seemed to be motivated mainly by greed and sex. The Americans had provided them with a slush fund, routed via their own authorities, to cover expenses - mainly bribes - but by the time Harper linked up with them, they already seemed to have spent most of it on alcohol and prostitutes. However, they knew the terrain they would be crossing and had had dealings with the drug lords he needed to meet, so he swallowed his reservations.

Although he was reliant on the Thais to navigate through the jungle of Myanmar to the RV with the drug lords, Harper had planned the route on the Thai side of the border himself.

They first drove north to Chiang Rai in two Toyota Landcruisers and overnighted at a colonial era hotel close to the river. He booked his own room for a month, cash in advance, and then told the manager 'I'll be keeping very irregular hours and I do not want to be disturbed at any time, for any reason, by chambermaids or anybody else during my stay. I hope we're clear on that, because the consequences for anyone who goes against those instructions will be very severe.' He slid a hundred dollar bill across the reception desk. 'Just to cover any extra trouble you have to go to,' he said.

The manager pocketed the tip with practised ease, while maintaining a neutral expression. 'As you wish sir, have a pleasant stay.'

While the Thais went looking for local girls from whom they could buy sex for the price of a meal, Harper began stashing the rest of his equipment in the room, including his gold chain and bug-out bag, and his burner phone. The phone would be of no use to him in the deep jungle and mountainous terrain of Myanmar - there would not be a mobile phone mast in a hundred miles - and he did not trust the Thai soldiers enough to dangle the temptation of a gold chain in front of them. He had transferred the bearer bonds in a sealed, air- and water-tight folder inside his backpack.

The next morning, he set a couple of traps to detect if anyone had been in his room while he was away. Normally he would have put a couple of corn-flakes or a cracker under the carpet. If they had been crushed when he checked them later, it would show there had been an intruder. However the hotel was crawling with cockroaches and he suspected that anything edible left there would have been eaten long before he got back. Instead he fixed a hair across the wardrobe door, and smeared a trace of Vaseline on the handles of the room and bathroom doors. If anyone touched them, even wearing gloves, there would be a mark.

Before setting out, he taped the folder containing the bearer bonds to his chest, under his shirt. A body search would reveal it in seconds but it was safer than carrying the bonds in the backpack. Then he locked his room and hid the key behind a ventilation grille high up in the wall at the far end of the corridor.

Harper and his crew then drove another 60 kilometres north to Mae Sai, a dusty, rugged, Wild West frontier town at the northernmost point of Thailand. It was deep inside the Golden Triangle, the one million square kilometre area spanning the confluence of the Mekong and Ruak rivers and the borders of Thailand, Laos and Myanmar. At one time it was the source of 70 per cent of the world's supply of heroin, and though the governments of the three countries had now supposedly cracked down on the heroin trade, the Golden Triangle was still awash with the drug. Corrupt Thai, Laotian and Burmese generals were heavily involved in the trade, with the Burmese military controlling their share through an apparently legitimate corporation - Myanmar Gas and Petrochemicals. The company had virtually no oil or gas or any other visible assets, yet strangely enough, every year hundreds of millions of dollars were laundered through its multiple bank accounts in the no-questions-asked state of Singapore.

Mae Sai faced the Burmese town of Tachileik across the Mae Sai River. It was one of only three official crossing points between Thailand and Myanmar and in this remote and lawless region it was the principal route by which smuggled goods of all sorts crossed the frontier. People traffickers brought in cheap or even slave labour from Myanmar for unscrupulous Thai factory owners; corrupt gem dealers smuggled "blood" rubies, sapphires, jade and ivory; and illegal logging companies shipped thousands of tons of teak, mahogany and other hardwoods through Mae Sai. However, by far the biggest trade was in the opium and heroin base that was processed, cut and repackaged in Thailand before being shipped on to the First World countries in Europe and the USA, where the appetite for the drug was never sated. Corrupt Burmese and Thai generals either ran the trade themselves or exacted a heavy price to look the other way while the goods crossed their territories.

Harper and his escort left their Landcruisers in a farm on the outskirts of town, and he paid the farmer the equivalent of six month's income to watch over the vehicles for them. Where they were going there were no roads that even a 4x4 could navigate, just a network of smugglers' paths and tracks that could only be negotiated by horse, mule or on foot. Although the officials on both sides of the border were notoriously corrupt and a bribe of a few dollars would probably have been enough to see them waved across the frontier, Harper preferred not to advertise their presence and instead he and his Thai escort crossed the Mae Sai river a couple of miles upstream of the town, using a inflatable boat that they deflated and sank after reaching Myanmar.

All of the men were armed with M16s. The Vietnam War had ended more than forty years before, but the American weapons of choice then, used by US troops and their South Vietnamese allies, had been the M16. Stolen or abandoned by the million during the course of the war and especially in the chaos of the US withdrawal, they could still be bought for a few dollars almost anywhere in South-East Asia and they were also better suited to the typically slight frames of Thai soldiers, than the much heavier AK47s and AK74s - the Kalashnikovs that were also widely available throughout the region.

They travelled through the foothills of the mountains, with the Thais leading the way, following tracks they had evidently used many times before. However, partly from habit and partly from his instinct for self-preservation, Harper also kept a close eye on the route they were following, noting compass bearings and identifying distinguishing landmarks he could use to navigate if he became separated from his escort. He never let his backpack out of his sight and whenever they paused to rest, he used it as a pillow.

They were now deep in a territory where the Burmese warlords and their allies in the military controlled everything. Once dense rainforest, the area was now scarred by logging, most of it illegal, that had stripped virtually a vast area of its tree cover, leaving only clumps of fern, bamboo and jungle thorn. Harper and the Thais lay up through part of the day, watching as teams of soldiers wearing the uniforms of the Burmese army, felled yet more giant teaks and other hardwood trees.

'How do they get the logs out?' Harper asked Narong.

'They're taken into Thailand through Mae Sai. Documentation is produced that shows they are legally felled trees from Thai forests, and then they're sold to the Japanese to make into chopsticks.'

'Chopsticks?' Harper said. 'You're kidding aren't you? Some of the world's most precious hardwoods and they're making them into something that's used once and then thrown away? And meanwhile back here-' he gestured towards the erosion scars on the hillsides, '-the lack of tree cover lets the monsoon rains rip away the topsoil and flood the lowlands. Still, as long as the generals are making a few bucks...' He shrugged. 'Forget it. It's none of my business. I'm just bumping my gums.'

As they moved deeper into Myanmar, they reached areas where the native rainforest was largely intact - for the moment at least. The jungle and the rugged terrain they were now crossing was traversed by a network of narrow tracks, barely wide enough for a man to pass. At intervals, alerted by the alarm cries of birds and animals in the jungle canopy above them, or the noise made by approaching men, Harper and his escort went to ground, while human "mule trains" - lines of peasants all stooped under the weight of the heavy packs they were carrying - made their way through the jungle, carrying raw opium down from the fields and hillsides where it was grown to the crude jungle "refineries" where it would be processed into heroin base.

There were also occasional patrols of Burmese soldiers, but although they were operating on their own terrain, they were ill-disciplined, poorly equipped and seemingly poorly schooled in jungle craft, for the noise they made and the smell of their tobacco smoke announced their presence long before they appeared, making it easy for Harper and the Thais to evade them.

Three days after crossing the border, they came to a broad valley right in the middle of the Golden Triangle, with small side-valleys running into the hills, matching the satellite imagery Harper had been shown by Button. There was a small hut on the upper slopes of the valley, where he and his Thai escort were to stay while he completed the negotiations with the local warlords. There was tinned food and bottled water, a case of the local Mekong whiskey, a generator for light and even two whores with dead eyes, sallow skin and track marks on their arms, who were soon being kept busy by the Thais. The diesel fuel for the generator and all the other supplies had been carried into the valley by the same human pack mules that took the raw opium away.

The next morning, Harper was introduced to the local warlords: four Burmese men, all with elaborate tattoos in traditional designs which they believed gave them mystical powers and could even protect them from knives and bullets. Each warlord also had his own retinue of ragged but heavily armed followers. They gave him the full guided tour, showing him the fruits of that year's poppy harvest, stored in five large bamboo barns spaced at intervals of a kilometre along the floor of the valley and hidden from aerial surveillance by tall forest trees that, unlike many other parts of this blighted region, had been left standing.

The barns were built on stilts for ventilation, with the peasants who picked the harvest living in the cramped space beneath the raised floors. Long ago, in more tranquil times, the barns had been used only to store the rice crop, and Burma, as it was then called, was a net exporter of rice to other countries. Now Myanmar imported most of the rice its often malnourished people ate, and the barns were used only to store the opium crop. The first three were already filled to the rafters with poppy husks - the poppies couldn't be converted into heroin until after the husks had ripened and the petals had dropped - and while Harper was there, peasants were trekking to and from the remaining barns, labouring to bring in the rest of the harvest.

At the end of the tour, Harper sat down with the warlords. His task was straightforward: to satisfy himself that they would hold up their end of the bargain and then hand over the $10 million deposit and discuss the means and timetable for arranging the destruction of the opium crop in return for a much larger US payment. The discussions were interminable, with long pauses each time the Thais translated his words and the warlords' replies. They appeared amicable enough, offering him tea and the clove-scented cigarettes they smoked but Harper had begun to feel a growing sense of unease. He could not put his finger on any specific reason for it but he had long since learned to trust his instincts and was already looking for a way to extricate himself and the Thais without triggering a full-scale gun-battle with the warlords' gangs.

His attention was focussed on the warlords in front of him, while the Thai special forces guys stood behind him to watch his back. The warlords were showing mounting impatience as Harper tried to establish how the destruction of the crop and the payments to them could be co-ordinated. It could only be done in phases, since neither side was willing to take the other side's compliance with the terms of their agreement on trust and eventually they reached an impasse. The senior warlord kept demanding that Harper pay them up front 'as a sign of your good faith', but he remained insistent that the bonds would only be handed over once all was in readiness for the destruction of the crop.

In the ensuing silence, he saw the main warlord give an almost imperceptible nod to Narong, who was standing directly behind Harper. At once he heard the click of a safety catch and felt the barrel of an M-16 assault rifle pressing against the back of his neck. From the corner of his eye, he saw that the other Thais had also brought their weapons to bear, not on the warlords, but on Harper. Surrounded and hugely outnumbered, he knew he was powerless to help himself.

While the others kept him covered, two of the Thais and the warlords' men then went through his backpack and equipment, ripping out the lining and cutting everything to shreds. Finding nothing, they then body-searched him and discovered the folder containing the bonds. The warlords broke into broad grins, passing them round and peering at the words and images engraved on them. Harper had a faint hope that they might fall out over the division of the spoils, since ten bearer bonds would not divide equally into four, but that disappeared as the main warlord handed one to each of the others three and one to Narong, and then pocketed the other six himself. Whatever their private thoughts might have been, none of the others showed even a flicker of protest at the unequal distribution.

At a word from the main warlord, the Thai soldiers had stripped Harper and removed his boots. It was a trick they used against Westerners because their soft feet meant that they couldn't run away without their boots. The warlords' plan was now obvious to him: they and their Thai allies had never had any serious intention of striking a deal to swap their crop for the bearer bonds; they were going to pocket the ten million dollars and as much extra money as they could persuade the Americans to part with and then go ahead and sell the opium crop anyway.

They began demanding that Harper tell them where the rest of the money was for the purchase of the heroin crop. When he denied any knowledge of it, they began to beat him. Narong and Decha repeatedly lashed his back and the soles of his feet with rattan canes, pausing only to ask him again and again. 'Where have you hidden the other bonds?'

'They're still at the American Embassy in Bangkok,' he said. 'You don't think I'd walk into a bear-trap naked do you? The $10 million was just a down payment and it's all I was entrusted with. If you want any more American money, you'll have to set me free and agree to the destruction of the harvest. No agreement, no money.'

They kept him there for two days and nights, depriving him of sleep, holding him in stress positions, beating and torturing him repeatedly, but Harper had not only gone through Resistance To Interrogation training in his days in the Paras, he was also a far more single-minded, stubborn and determined individual than any of his captors had ever met and they could not break him down.

By then the Thais appeared to have given up hope of getting any more money from the Americans. It was clear to Harper that Narong just wanted to kill him, before returning to Thailand with some cover story of being ambushed and losing Harper in a firefight, but the main warlord had other ideas. 'If we can't have the rest of the bonds,' he said to Harper, in broken English, 'we can still sell our opium crop and we can also send you back to your Western masters with a message.' He gestured to one of his men, pressing his thumb against his first two fingers and the next moment Harper was pinned to the dirt floor of the hut. A cord was jerked tight round his arm, and he watched in helpless, absolute terror as Decha approached with a filthy syringe, found a vein in Harper's arm and injected him with heroin. As the cord was untied, he felt the rush and fell back, eyes unseeing, lost in the drug. He'd heard heroin users describe the feeling as being 'better than sex, better than anything,' now, feeling it for himself for the first time, he could understand why they would make those comparisons.

Time ceased to have any meaning for him. Every time he came back to his senses after that, still lying on the dirt floor of the hut, sometimes in daylight, sometimes at night, one of the warlords' men injected him again. Narong, Decha and the other Thais had disappeared, presumably returning to Bangkok. Harper lost all track of how many days - or was it weeks - he had been held there, existing only in a heroin haze, each day identical to the one before. He was dimly aware of glimpses of the steady procession of peasants trudging to and from the storage barns with huge sacks of opium poppyheads on their backs, but each time his captors saw that he was awake and aware of his surroundings, they pinned him down and gave him another fix of heroin. He no longer struggled or tried to resist, but let the heroin silence the tremors and the cravings that now ruled his body, drowning every other thought but the next fix.

One day apparently no different from the others, the main warlord and his men took Harper out of the hut where they'd been holding him and marched him back down the valley towards the Thai border. They had to support him much of the time, because he was so weak he could barely walk.

They stopped at the ridge overlooking the Mae Sai river. 'Okay, big man,' the warlord said to him. 'You go back to Thailand and then give Uncle Sam a message from us. Tell him we rule South-east Asia now. If he sends any more round-eyes here, it will be like Vietnam all over again - we'll kill them all.'

His men pushed a bag of heroin and a hypodermic into Harper's hands and then disappeared back into the jungle. By then he had such bad withdrawal symptoms that he shot up before they were even out of sight.

Chapter 3

Somehow Harper managed to get back across the border after dark that night. He found what appeared to be the only available internet in Mae Sai, in a combination bar, general store and smugglers' hang-out that had four battered computer terminals set up on a wooden bench against one wall, in full view of everyone in the room. Harper sold half of his remaining heroin to one of the crooks lounging at the bar and used some of the cash to buy some internet time. He hunched over the terminal, blocking the view of the screen while he logged in to the email account he used to communicate with Button. It was painfully slow to load, but eventually he was able to leave a four-word message in the Drafts folder: "Meet Chiang Rai urgentest". Identifying the place where they would meet in the Drafts folder was a risk, albeit a very slight one, that he would not normally have taken, but this was a desperate situation.

He bought a bowl of rice and a stew so thin it was more like soup, then set out at once for Chiang Rai. The Thais had taken the Landcruiser from the farm where he had left it, but he walked out to Highway 1 and managed to flag down a truck heading south with a load of teak logs. He used the rest of his baht to bribe the driver to take him to Chiang Rai. By the time the trucker dropped him there, Harper was again in deep withdrawal, his hands trembling and his body pouring with sweat. He shot up with a little more of his dwindling store of heroin, then headed for the hotel where he had stashed his bug-out bag and the remainder of his kit. The key was still behind the ventilation grille and none of the "tells" he had set inside the room had been disturbed.

He grabbed a thick handful of baht from his bug-out bag and hurried to an internet cafe to check for Button's response. She was arriving in Chiang Rai that night, flying in on a Nok Air flight from Bangkok. He left directions to an RV, bought some food and then headed out onto the streets of the town to score more heroin. It didn't prove hard to do for half the population of Chiang Rai appeared to be involved with the heroin trade in one way or another.

Button arrived that night, driven into town from the airport in a decrepit Mercedes taxi that must have had at least a quarter of a million miles on the clock. While Harper carried out counter-surveillance, she walked the route he had prescribed for her. She was clearly well out of her comfort zone, for he could see that her eyes were darting everywhere and she was jumping at every movement in the darkness around her.

When he was satisfied that she hadn't been followed, Harper appeared out of the shadows and took her to his hotel. 'My God, Lex,' she said, as he closed the door of his room and turned to face her. 'Look at the state of you. What the hell happened?'

'It's a long story, Charlie, but basically we've been double-crossed. The Thais were in league with the warlords and neither of them were really interested in doing the deal. They just wanted to take the bonds and then sell the crop anyway. I was lucky to get away. So, we're going to need to move to Plan B and destroy the crop without the warlords' cooperation. Air strikes won't do it without target-marking because the barns and store places are too well concealed. So I need you to get me some kit and then I'll be heading back in to finish the job. I'll mark the targets and then call in the air strikes.'

'Is that wise?'

'Possibly not, but I'm going to do it anyway. And it has to be now before the harvest is finished and they begin to move the crop across the border. If that happens, the opportunity to destroy it will be gone.'

'And your opportunity for revenge gone with it, Lex?'

There was a long silence before he replied. 'I never like leaving a job half done but in this case, you're right, it's also personal - very personal. I need to do this.' He paused again. 'There's one more thing you should know, Charlie.' He pulled back his sleeves and showed her the track marks on his arms. 'They gave me something to remember them by. They shot me full of heroin over and over again. So I'm now a full-blown addict.'

'Oh my God.'

'Don't worry, I'm going to get clean, but it'll take time and there's a debt I need to repay first.'

'Bloody hell, Lex, forget about that. We've got to get you off that stuff before you do anything else. I'll find some people who can help.'

'That'll be great when the time's right, but that isn't now. Those barns were filling up with the last of the opium crop. Once the harvest's all in, they'll be moving it out. There's no time to waste.'

'But you're hooked on heroin, Lex.'

'I can control it.'

'Isn't that what all addicts say?'

'Maybe, but addicts tend to have fucked up lives that give them a reason not to give up smack - I don't. And addicts don't have my willpower either. I've already thought it through. I'll use enough heroin to keep me functioning while I do the job and then when it's over I can go cold turkey and clean up.'

She gave him a dubious look.

'It'll work, Charlie. How many rock musicians have been functioning on heroin for years?'

'But they're only playing gigs and making albums, they're not trying to cross a hundred miles of hostile territory and then launch a precision attack.'

'It'll work. You'll just have to trust me on that. Now even if I wasn't on smack, I couldn't carry enough demolition kit to destroy that crop. In fact even a battalion of men couldn't carry enough kit for that. So I'll be placing TMTs - Target Marking Transmitters - that you'll need to get for me. I'll leave you to make the necessary arrangements with the cousins but, beginning three days from now, I need the Yanks to be standing by at dawn every morning with Cruise missiles, Warthog tank-busters, B-52s or whatever they're going to use to destroy the crop, waiting for me to call in the air strikes. So from you I need the TMTs, some more cash and some other kit and weapons, including some comms, a rifle and some armour-piercing, tracer rounds, and obviously everything needs to be untraceable.'

'Obviously.' She folded her arms and clearly wasn't happy.

'And I need it all here inside 24 hours. Can you do it?'

'I'll do my best. Give me the list and I'll have it couriered to you by the time you're eating your breakfast. Then I'll be flying back to London.'

'Plausible deniability?' he said.

'The best kind.'

He scribbled a list of what he needed and handed it to her. She got ready to leave but then paused in the doorway and gave him a searching look. 'You're sure you can do this, Lex?'

He spread his hands. 'Have I ever failed you?'

'Not yet, but there's always a first time, and you've never been a smack addict before.'

She closed the door and a couple of minutes later he heard a taxi pull-up outside. Button was on her way back to the airport for the last flight of the day to Bangkok.

Harper took some more money from his bug-out bag and in a dive bar in the roughest part of town he scored even more heroin, enough to get him in and out of Myanmar again. He wasn't hungry but he made himself eat and then lay down to rest, though the junk in his system made it a short and troubled night. Early the next morning he bought another Landcruiser from the same dealer he had used before, who showed no visible surprise or interest at the same customer buying two cars in the space of a fortnight.

At eleven that morning, a black Range Rover with diplomatic plates pulled up outside the hotel and two burly Caucasians, one of them pulling a wheeled suit-case, walked through the lobby and took the stairs to Harper's room. They handed him the case and left without exchanging a word.

When he opened the case, he found that Button had not only come up with the TMTs and some comms equipment, but a couple of vintage and untraceable souvenirs left over from the US involve-ment in Vietnam: a Browning automatic rifle and a box of ammunition stamped "APTP": Armour Piercing Tracer Phosphorous. There was also a box of standard rounds. He spent an hour stripping, cleaning and re-assembling the rifle and checking the rest of the equipment. He packed it into a bergen with some rations and the rest of his heroin, then loaded the Landcruiser and drove north.

He made a clandestine crossing of the border and, using every scrap of field-craft he'd learned in his career, and the landmarks and compass bearings he'd noted on his way into Myanmar with Narong and Decha and their men, managed to follow the same route to the warlords' base deep in the Burmese jungle. On the ridge overlooking the hut where he'd been held, he made a hide beneath a banana plant, so the leaves would hide him from sight and protect him from the sun, in case he had to be there a long time. Then he shot up with heroin again. He wasn't happy about using the drug but he knew that now was not the time to be going cold turkey.

Shortly before last light he prayed to the only god he recognised - the god of vengeance - and then made his way down into the valley. One of the warlord's men was standing guard on the first of the storage barns, but he was half-asleep and easy to evade as Harper circled around and placed a TMT close to the rear of the barn. It was no bigger than a matchbook and very easy to conceal.

He placed one at each of the other barns and was just siting the last one when he heard the cry of a baby from the opium pickers' primitive living quarters under the barn. It was choked off almost at once, as the child found its mother's breast and began to suckle, but it echoed in his mind all the way back up the side of the valley. He had to harden his heart before he sent a single burst transmission on his radio, then lay down to wait for daybreak.

He was still wide-awake when dawn came up over the valley; the adrenaline and the heroin in his veins saw to that. One of the warlord's men came out onto the veranda and stood watching the sunrise. Harper glanced at his watch, then fired one round and the man leapt backwards through the door. Harper smiled to himself. It was exactly what he wanted him to do.

He put his next shot into the fuel tank at the side of the hut. The burning tracer etched the track of the round across the valley and it went through the quarter-inch mild steel like a welder's torch, causing fuel to spurt out, but he had fired too low; even a tracer phosphorus round won't ignite liquid diesel. He put the next shot a little higher, aiming for the fuel-air vapour above the liquid and this time, as the shot hit home, the tank erupted in a ball of flame. It vaporised the hut and the warlords' men inside it. By now, the shots and the explosion had roused the whole valley. As Harper had hoped, the peasants and their families, including several women with babies in their arms, were now streaming from under the storage barns and running for the safety of the hills, but the warlords' men remained behind, buzzing around the barns like angry hornets, still uncertain from where the attack had come.

Two minutes passed. Harper checked his watch again, then turned his back to the valley, put his fingers in his ears and opened his mouth wide to equalise the pressure and protect his ears and lungs from the blast waves that he knew were coming. With his mouth closed, his lungs could rupture from the overpressure and then the sudden drop in pressure following a blast, and without his fingers in his ears, his eardrums might burst.

There was a few seconds pause and then a Whoosh! of disturbed air and the first barn disintegrated in a massive fireball. The other four followed within a heartbeat as cruise missiles fired from American warships in the Indian Ocean tracked along the transmitter beams from the TMTs Harper had sited and detonated in the core of each building. A succession of blast waves swept over him, rattling his teeth as a storm of dust, debris and shredded leaves and palm fronds whirled around him. When the smoke and dust cleared, there was nothing taller than a toothpick along the whole valley floor. The warlords had used Harper to send a message to Uncle Sam. This was the reply.

Harper had a brief thought about searching for some of the bearer bonds, but if they were still on the warlord's body they would have been incinerated along with him when the Cruise missiles detonated, and if they were hidden somewhere there was no hope finding them. He packed up his kit and began to trek back towards the border. He took a very circuitous route, first heading north, directly away from the border and then looping around to make his way south again, being careful to leave no sign as he did so. He was still travelling with maximum care to be sure of avoiding any patrols sent out by the surviving warlords to intercept those responsible for the destruction of their entire opium crop.

Before nightfall that day, the US President had made a televised broadcast to the nation, boasting 'My fellow Americans, we have dealt a blow to the international heroin trade that they will never recover from,' and showing satellite imagery of the devastated area.

Harper crossed the frontier safely and made his way back to Pattaya. His first port of call was Bee's internet café. He logged onto the email account and opened the latest draft message from Charlotte Button.

'You're a conquering hero, Lex,' said her message. 'The Americans are over the moon.'

He smiled to himself and typed out a message. 'There's just one problem, Charlie. I'm a conquering hero who also happens to be a junkie. Can you imagine how that feels? For the first time in my entire life I've come up against something that I'm afraid may be stronger than me, physically and mentally. I just hope I can beat it.' He stared at the message for several seconds and then deleted it. He typed out a second message. 'Just make sure the money goes into my bank account,' he said. And then he added a smiley face for good measure.

Chapter 4

Harper went back to his apartment and gave himself just enough of a fix to stave off the tremors for a while and then sent a text from one of his burner phones. While he was waiting for help to arrive in answer to his summons, he left his apartment and, paying cash, a month in advance, he rented an empty shop with a stone cellar beneath it, in an outlying district. The cellar was piled with rubbish dumped by the previous tenant of the shop but devoid of furniture. The only break in the stone walls was a tiny, steel-barred window high up in the outer wall. The thick glass was almost opaque with cobwebs and dirt but peering upwards, he could dimly make out the shape of people's legs and feet as they passed along the street outside.

He drove to a supermarket and bought the supplies he thought he would need: a five gallon container, a pair of buckets with lids, cheap towels, packs of tissues, flat breads, oranges, mangoes and bananas, energy drinks to replenish his electrolytes, soda water to combat nausea, and a pack of Imodium to deal with one of the many unpleasant side-effects of what he was about to do.

He cleared out the rubbish from the cellar and put a mattress and a couple of blankets on the floor. He filled the five gallon container with water and put it with the rest of his supplies next to the head of the mattress but he sited the lidded buckets in the opposite corner, as far from the food and water as possible. Having stacked up all his purchases, he then escape-proofed the cellar by removing the inside handle and strengthening the door by bolting stout hardwood planks to it. He finished by cutting a small hole no bigger than a cat flap near the bottom of the door with a hinged, lockable hatch on the outside.

In response to his text, Maggie May arrived within 24 hours. A pale, dark-eyed brunette in her thirties, she was a surveillance professional who had once worked for MI5, also known as "Box 500". At one time the agency's postal address had been PO Box 500, and though that had long since changed, the code-name "Box 500" or just plain "Box" had never been abandoned. Her MI5 career had come to an abrupt halt after an affair with her boss led to her becoming pregnant. Although her public school educated boss would never have expressed it quite so inelegantly, his reaction to her news boiled down to an ultimatum: 'Get an abortion or get a new job'. As Maggie May herself remarked, without too obvious a trace of bitterness, 'That's what you get for sleeping with your boss: pregnant and fired.'

She had chosen the second option and was now the single mother of a young son. Harper had been very glad to hire her. She was a trusted member of his regular team of surveillance and intelligence-gathering professionals, but he also used her as a mentor and sounding board as well as for her particular skills. Whenever he called her with the offer of a job, she was able to leave her boy with her mother, who thought she worked as a rep for a travel company. It gave her a convincing reason for her need to make frequent trips abroad. The money Harper paid her for previous jobs had already given her and her son financial security, but she carried on working for him mainly because she loved the work.

Harper came straight to the point. 'This is going to be a bit outside the normal comfort zones for both of us because the only surveillance I'll need you to be carrying out is on me.'

He told her the problem.

'What does it feel like when you're high?' she asked.

'It's ...' He paused struggling for the words. 'It's the best feeling you've ever experienced in your life; you're drowning in dopamine, so of course you feel that way and that's why people use it. And when you begin to come down from it, your first thought is just "Where can I get some more?". But if you can cast a cold eye on it, you know it's all fake - just chemicals overloading the receptors your brain - and if you look around you, you realise that you're knee deep in shit, and you'll die if you don't do something about it.'

'So what's the solution?'

'I'm going to lock myself in the cellar and go cold turkey. Your job is to keep me fed and watered, and keep an eye on me. If it's necessary - and I mean only as an absolute last resort, not just because I've got bad withdrawal symptoms - you can call in outside medical help. Okay?'

He waited for her nod before continuing. 'I'll make the usual payment to your offshore bank, and the duties shouldn't be too arduous, though I don't know what this is going to be like and I can't imagine that it will be pretty to watch. Anyway, once I'm in there, I want you to lock the door behind me and whatever I say to you, whatever noises you hear, don't open it for a week, other than to give me fresh food and water and cast an eye over me every few hours. It's probably better if you stay away most of the time. Just come back and check up on me and open the hatch once a day, pass some fresh water and plenty of fruit and bread through it and then close and lock it again.'

'It all seems a bit extreme,' she said.

'Does it? Well that's because I'm trying to deal with an extreme problem.'

'But does it have to be cold turkey like this? Can't you get some proper medical help?'

'What and get addicted to methadone instead? No thanks, it has to be this way. Cold turkey.'

'Why do they call it that?' she asked.

He smiled ruefully. 'Because one of the symptoms when you stop taking smack abruptly is that you get goose pimples on your skin, so you look just like a plucked, uncooked turkey.'

She shook her head. 'Your ability to come up with irrelevant fascinating facts at moments of crisis never ceases to amaze me, Lex, but can we focus on the here and now? I've seen you solve a lot of problems, win a lot of fights and take out a lot of bad guys over the years, but this time your adversary is yourself. So can you do it?'

'I reckon so. And I'm not fighting myself, I'm fighting the heroin addiction that's poisoning me. Obviously it's uncharted territory for me - nothing in all the fighting and training I've done addresses this - but junkies get addicted because they don't like their lives. I love mine, so I'll do what it takes to get it back. I've also got some unfinished business to take care of, which should be an extra incentive.' He paused, studying her expression. 'Right, are you good to go?'

'Already?'

'No time like the present.'

'Yes, if you're sure.'

'I'm sure, no sense waiting. Any last words?'

'Just be sure and come back out of there. Oh and Lex? I know enough medicine to know that, just like when you're dealing with a hangover, the liver is the organ that will do the heavy lifting to metabolise and eliminate the toxins - the heroin - in your system. So you need to take care of your liver by keeping your fluid intake high. If you're vomiting or get diarrhoea, you'll dehydrate rapidly, so make yourself keep taking fluids.'

He gave her a wink. 'Got it.' He grinned. 'Maybe you could wear a sexy nurse's uniform to cheer me up?'

'Or maybe I could just kick you in the nuts.'

They both laughed, then she stepped forward and impulsively hugged him.

Before he went into the cellar, he flushed the rest of his stash of heroin down the toilet, snapped the needle of his syringe and dumped it in the trash with his tie-belt, lighter and the rest of his "works". There was the trace of a tremor in his voice as he said 'Well, see you on the other side then,' but he squared his shoulders, walked into the cellar and closed the door behind him.

He waited until he heard the sound of the key turning in the lock, then lay down on the mattress, closed his eyes and tried to rest. He knew that withdrawal symptoms would begin within a few hours of the last fix so he would soon be gripped by them. He had only the vaguest of ideas about what to expect. He'd read a couple of newspaper articles about addiction and seen *Trainspotting* at the movies but he doubted it would be much guide to what he would experience and he certainly wasn't expecting to see a baby crawling across the ceiling and down the walls. He pushed the thought away, closed his eyes and waited.

The minutes crawled by and despite trying to clear his mind, slow his pulse rate and zone out, every sense was on alert for the least tremor or feeling that might mark the start of the real withdrawal symptoms. He did not have long to wait.

The first signs could merely have been symptoms of his anxious state, but he was beginning to feel ever more restless, nervous and agitated, and found it almost impossible to lie or sit still. He began pacing up and down his self-imposed cell, but six paces took him the length of the cellar, and it was just four from one side to the other. He tried to delay looking at his watch for as long as possible; when he eventually did so, he found that barely two hours had passed since Maggie May had locked the door on him. He glanced up towards the tiny barred window and saw the already dim light through it was fading still more as night came on.

If there was one thing he missed about England apart from the changing seasons, it was the soft evening light as the sun sank below the horizon and the dusk slowly darkened the sky. On this night he missed it more than ever. In the tropics there was no gentle transition from day to night; as soon as the sun went down, night came on with a rush and tonight promised to be the longest he had ever spent.

He heard the rattle of the hatch and Maggie May's voice. 'All right Lex?'

'Yes. I'll find it easier if you leave me alone. Just stick to what we agreed.'

'If you're sure?'

He didn't reply and after a few seconds the hatch was closed and locked. He felt bad for the abrupt way he'd spoken to her, but a sympathetic voice was not what he wanted to hear and he was afraid that every time she opened the hatch, it would just increase the temptation to find reasons for her to release him straight away.

As the evening wore on, his restlessness increased and he was also now suffering symptoms that in other circumstances he would have put down to flu. His eyes and nose were streaming, his joints and muscles were aching, a headache was pounding in his temples and every few minutes a violent bout of shivering shook him. He lay down on the mattress and tried to rest but within minutes he was back on his feet and pacing the cellar.

The night was interminable. When he lay down and tried to rest, muscle spasms set him twitching and cursing, and waves of nausea were sweeping over him. On the one occasion he did manage to drift off to sleep for a few minutes, he woke from a nightmare, eyes wild and staring, to find the mattress drenched in his sweat and his heart beating so fast that his pulse was beating in his ears like a snare drum banging in six-eight time.

The cravings for the drug were now so intense that he found himself wanting a fix more than anything he had wanted in his whole life. In his more lucid moments he kept reminding himself that the obsession dominating his every thought wasn't really what he wanted, it was just the drug refusing to give up its hold without a fight. Well, he'd fought often enough in other circumstances, surely he could win a fight with himself as well. He tried to summon happy memories to counter the sick depression that was threatening to overwhelm him, but all he could dredge up were dark thoughts that grew bleaker and bleaker as the night progressed. At one point he even found himself pounding on the door and yelling to Maggie May. 'I've changed my mind, get me out of here. You hear me? Get me out!' But either she wasn't there or she had heeded his instructions to ignore any noises from the other side of the cellar door.

As the dawn light at last began to show, his cravings for the drug were augmented by a feeling of blind, furious rage. The faintest noise filtering to him from the street outside as the city came to life drove him mad with irritation. He was grinding his teeth so hard that his gums were bleeding, but he could not stop himself and the noise was so loud in his head that he began to punch the wall, using the pain to try and drown the sound.

Just as he felt he was beginning to get control of his fury, those symptoms began to subside and a fresh wave hit him: this time such powerful feelings of dizziness and nausea that he could no longer stand up and had to slump onto his mattress. He lay there, his head spinning, gagging and dry heaving, and then he began to vomit. For hour after hour, long after his stomach had been purged of everything it had contained, he continued to puke and dry heave.

As the urge to vomit finally began to abate, he slumped back on his stained, filthy mattress, closed his eyes and for a few minutes may even have fallen asleep, but the next phase was now creeping up on him. He woke feeling as if ants were crawling over his skin. The sensation was so real that he tried to brush them off him, but then the ants began to bite, he felt stinging sensations all over his body and when he lifted his arm he could see - or imagined that he could - the red bodies of fire ants, their mandibles biting into his skin. He shouted and yelled, scratching furiously at his arms as he tried to dislodge them, but that only made the feeling worse. He stumbled to his feet, blundering into the wall, and when he looked down he saw that he was scratching the track marks on his arms so hard that he had drawn blood. He pushed his hands into his pockets to stop him scratching himself and kept them there, even though the itching, stinging and biting sensations on his skin were almost unendurable.

As that began to fade, he drank a few mouthfuls of water, the first he had managed to keep down since the vomiting phase began. He lay down on the mattress and closed his eyes but at once, nightmares or hallucinations - he could no longer say whether he was awake or asleep - began to assail him. Whenever he closed his eyes a fresh horrific image filled his mind, so vivid it seemed absolutely real, jolting him upright with terror etched on his face.

There were nightmare visions of torture and deaths in which the faces of men he had killed - and there had been many of those - unseen for years and long forgotten, now again swam before him. Hands reached out for him, knives jabbed at him and the sound of gunfire, screams and cries jerked him back to consciousness whenever he managed to close his eyes. The things he saw seemed more real to him than the stone cellar where he lay, trapped with his nightmares. He began to question his own sanity and even briefly harboured thoughts of suicide to escape the torment he was enduring, but at once he pulled back from the brink as his iron will reasserted itself.

He knew that there would be no cavalry riding to his rescue, and though he had not put himself in this situation, only he could extricate himself from it. He reminded himself for the thousandth time that what he was seeing and feeling was not real, just the drug that had poisoned him and which was now fighting him for control of his mind and body. 'I'm going to get through this!' he shouted aloud, though his parched throat, swollen tongue and cracked lips made the voice almost unrecognisable as his.

When his symptoms permitted, he exercised furiously, knocking out press-ups and sit-ups by the hundred on the cold stone floor until he collapsed exhausted. At other times, he could only lie flat, grinding his teeth or pacing his cell, while either sweat poured from him in torrents, or chills and ferocious bouts of shivering set his teeth rattling in his head. He shouted, swore and at times begged and pleaded with Maggie May to 'open the door and get me a fix - just one more.'

Furious at his weakness in that moment, he abandoned every other thought to focus on one simple purpose: to survive, if only because he had too much burning hate for those who had done this to him to allow them to escape unscathed. That hate was a far more powerful motivation than any happy-clappy thoughts or memories he might have been able to conjure. He sat with his back against the wall, focussed his gaze on the opposite wall and sat there staring balefully at it. He refused to allow himself to rest and let every twitch, every spasm, fill him with ever more hatred.

He lost all track of time and was no longer sure if this was the second, third, fourth or fifth day he had been confined. Food and water came and went, the stinking buckets in the corner were still there, and the only thing that suggested time passing was that his symptoms were now beginning to ease a little. It was not a steady process; there were flashbacks and periods when he shook like a leaf in a gale, or tore at his skin with his nails, and again howled obscenities at the stone walls of his self-imposed prison. There were other times, however, when he was able to lie relatively still and close his eyes without summoning fresh horrors from his subconscious, and even snatch some precious sleep.

Badly shaken, Maggie May had tried to close her ears to the sounds from the other side of the cellar door and, as instructed, only opened the hatch to change his water and food, which was often left uneaten. On the third morning, deep in the depths of withdrawal, he had rushed to the hatch and tried to grab her wrist as she reached through to place a jug of fresh water on the floor. She cursed and snatched her hand away just in time. From then on, she kept well back from the hatch until she was sure that Harper was at the far side of the cellar or lying on his mattress, oblivious of her.

As the days went by, his hallucinations, chills, spasms and tremors eased still more and on the eighth day, when Maggie May opened the hatch to change his food and water, she saw him lying fast asleep and looking more relaxed than at any time since his withdrawal had begun. The next morning his food had all been eaten for the first time since he went in there. When she called to him, waking him from a sleep, he was pale, hollow-eyed and almost unrecognisable behind his nine-day growth of beard, but his voice was steadier and his hands no longer shook like leaves in a gale.

'How are you feeling?' she said.

'Better.' His voice was a harsh rasp.

'Well enough to be sprung from jail?'

He hesitated. 'Let's leave it one more day, just to be sure.'

When he emerged the next morning, he was so unsteady on his legs that Maggie May had to take his arm and help him up the cellar steps. She flagged down a tuk-tuk, took Harper back to his apartment and set up a plastic chair in the shower. Wrinkling her nose at the smell and ignoring his protests, she stripped him of his sweat-stained clothes and stuffed them into a bin-bag. 'Bloody hell, Lex,' she said. 'In my idle moments I have sometimes wondered what it would be like to rip the clothes off you, but none of my fantasies included this scenario.'

He smiled. 'Better wait until I'm in better condition before trying me out. If you've been dreaming about me all the time we've known each other, I'd hate it to be a disappointment when it finally happens.'

She laughed. 'Probably about the same time as hell freezes over, but meanwhile ...'

She sat him on the chair, handed him soap and shampoo and then switched on the shower. He sat there for twenty minutes, letting the water cascade over him, and then she towelled him dry and helped him into bed. He was asleep before she reached the door. While he slept, she went back to the empty shop and paid a couple of Thais she found squatting in the dust at the side of the street 1000 baht each to clean out the cellar and burn the mattress and all the other contents.

Harper slept for twenty-four hours straight and when he eventually woke he already looked more like his old self. He got up at once and went for a run along the beach, then ate enough breakfast for three men before beginning a gruelling routine to rebuild his strength and fitness, rotating between weights, running, huge meals and heavy sleep. At Maggie May's suggestion he also went for tests for HIV and hepatitis. 'Those dirty syringes may have been used by other addicts before you, Lex. You need to be sure.'

He went for the tests and though he affected to be unworried about them, Maggie May read the look in his eye and was not fooled. However when he returned, he was grinning broadly. 'I dropped lucky: all clear.'

They went out for dinner and drinks that night at a seafood restaurant off Walking Street, Harper treating her to what he described as 'the best meal in Pattaya accompanied by a bottle of ruinously expensive imported champagne, as a thank you for what you've done for me.'

She smiled. 'No thanks needed Lex, after all, you were paying me to be here, but I would have done it for nothing too. You've been good to me over the years and I owe you big time. I've been able to provide for my family and give my son the education I never had and that's all down to you.' She paused. 'You never talk about your own family, do you?'

There was a long silence which she broke in the end. 'See what I mean,' she said with a laugh.

Harper shrugged. 'There's nothing to talk about really. My mum died when I was a kid, my father didn't. If there was any justice in the world, it would have been the other way round. I ran away from home a few times.' He gave a bleak smile. 'That's probably where I learned my survival skills. Unarmed combat I learned from my father, and not in a good way. I was always in trouble and would probably have ended up in prison if I hadn't joined the army. So there you have it: all my family history that's fit to be told.'

She leaned forward and took his hand. 'Sorry, I shouldn't have pried.'

'I don't mind, but now it's your turn. Tell me about your parents. I know your mother looks after your boy when you're away, but I've never heard you talk about your father.'

'My father was in the forces too,' she said. 'He was an RAF helicopter pilot. He was shot down in Oman - one of those endless secret wars that the SAS was fighting in the Middle East and Far East back then. He survived but was taken prisoner by the insurgents they were fighting. I don't know what they did to him - he never, ever talked about it - but it marked him for life.'

She twisted a strand of hair at her temple around her finger as she spoke, her voice a monotone. 'When he was released, he was medically discharged from the Air Force. I used to watch, powerless to help or comfort him, as he sat for hour after hour in his chair at home, with tears rolling down his cheeks.'

She fell silent. She was still looking at Harper but he knew that it was not his face that she was seeing. 'One day - it was a Saturday in late autumn with the last leaves clinging to the trees - he was sitting staring out of the window while I did my homework at the table. We were alone in the house; my mother had gone shopping. He got up and walked over to where I was sitting and stood looking over my shoulder for a moment. Then he leaned forward, touched my hair and whispered, "Work hard. Make me proud of you." Then he went out through the kitchen into the garage and closed the door.'

Her voice cracked and tears again welled up in her eyes. 'He had a workbench out there. I thought he'd gone to fix something. My mother found him when she came back half an hour later. He'd hanged himself from a beam in the roof.'

Harper squeezed her hand. 'I'm so sorry.' He realised that there was nothing he could say that would make her feel better, but he felt her pain.

CHAPTER 5

For weeks afterwards, Harper felt returning flashes of his former craving for heroin but he never had the least temptation to use again. Even if he'd been put in an empty room with a stash of the drug, he would have flushed it away without a moment's pause. He had continued his punishing fitness regime and three weeks after he had emerged from the cellar where he'd gone cold turkey, he pronounced himself ready.

'Ready for what?' Maggie May said. He had phoned her on his burner mobile and she had clearly been pleased to hear from him. She had gone back to England a few days after he had emerged from the cellar, once she was sure that he had truly beaten his addiction.

'Ready for anything, but one thing in particular: tying up the loose ends from the job that got me hooked on smack in the first place.'

'Now why do I suspect that "tying up the loose ends" might be a bit of an understatement for what you've got in mind.'

He grinned. 'Because you know me so well.'

'Any more work for me in it?'

'I need someone to do surveillance with me, but if you want to stay with your boy I can-'

She cut him off. 'I miss him, of course, but he's fine with his grandmother. Talk me through the job.' She listened as he explained what he wanted to do. 'Bloody hell, Lex, that's quite a task you've set yourself,' she said. 'The place'll be protected by a lot more than a padlock and an entry phone, and they'll be armed like the Thai Army.'

'They're part of the Thai army - or were - so that's not too surprising,' he said. 'But even the whole of the Thai Army wouldn't stop me from getting to them. This is personal for me, but if you want out, that's fine - no complaints, no judgement from me, I already owe you big time for what you did for me.'

'Want out?' she said. 'I wouldn't miss it for the world. I'll be on the next plane out there.'

Harper also called in the help of another two regular members of his team. As usual, Hansfree, a pale, intense-looking man in his mid-thirties, arrived dressed all in black and wearing black leather gloves. The nickname, chosen by Hansfree himself, was in the blackest of black humour. It referred to the loss of both of his hands when an IED detonated as he was examining it. He was immune to feelings of self-pity, pointing out that he had been lucky to survive at all, and had made a nonsense of descriptions of his injuries as "a disability" by using his prosthetic hands, voice recognition software, his intelligence and his genius with computer technology, to become Harper's resident electronic wizard. There was nothing a two-handed person could do on a computer that Hansfree couldn't do just as well; and in fact he usually did it better and quicker too.

Harper also summoned another regular, who operated under the *nom de guerre* of Barry Big, or sometimes just BB. He was a bluff, blunt and powerfully-built man, a Yorkshireman and proud of it, who had been a member of the SRR - the Special Reconnaissance Regiment, the successor to 14 Int. He was a surveillance professional who also had the combat skills to fight his way out if he was compromised. He was now based in the Dominican Republic, the homeland of his partner. They owned a beachfront bar together, which she ran alone when he was away. She was younger than BB, very beautiful and didn't speak a word of English. He didn't speak Spanish either but, as he often said with a grin, 'one way and another, we seem to make ourselves understood.'

Forty-eight hours after he called them, they were in Pattaya ready to be briefed.

The combination of Hansfree's phone taps and email intercepts, Maggie May's expertise at eyes-on surveillance, and Barry Big's surveillance and combat experience, allied to Harper's formidable skill-set and his extensive network of contacts in the Thai underworld produced results within days. It turned out that Narong, Decha and their men, who had conspired to betray him to the Burmese warlords, were heavily involved in one of the biggest drug packaging operations in Bangkok. The heroin base had been processed into pure heroin at crude factories deep in the Thai jungle near the border with Myanmar, but it was then shipped to Bangkok to be repackaged for export. The repackaging was done in a razor wire encircled compound on the outskirts of the city. The heroin was packed into crates labelled as machine parts, drums of industrial chemicals, white goods like washing machines and a multitude of other, apparently innocent cargoes and loaded into shipping containers. They were then shipped by air or sea to dealers operating in every First World country. Not every consignment got through, but it was impossible for Customs and narcotics officers to check more than a tiny proportion of the enormous volumes of goods passing daily through their ports and airports, and the profits for the drug traffickers were so enormous that the loss of an occasional shipment was just treated as part of the cost - and a very minor one at that - of doing business.

Another heroin packaging operation was being run from a fourth floor apartment in Khlong Toei, the district of Bangkok that tourists rarely ever saw, where he had first met up with Narong and his men. It was armoured like Fort Knox - steel grilles on the windows, steel shutters on the doors, heavily armed guards on the entrances and exits, and a network of look-outs in the surrounding streets, reporting back sightings of any unknown faces or strange vehicles before they could get within half a mile of the place.

Harper had rented a safe house a mile away from the apartment, far enough from it that there was no danger of being spotted or compromised by the Thais or their look-outs. He paid three months rent in advance, in cash, and brought in all the weapons and equipment he thought he would need. However, before he could risk an attack on the apartment, he had to have detailed knowledge of its barriers to entry - alarms, booby-traps, guard routines - and the escape routes those inside would use in the event of a raid by police or rival traffickers, or a fire or other emergency. Surveillance, phone-taps, email intercepts and sigint - signals intelligence - could only take him so far. What he needed now was humint - human intelligence - and the only way to obtain that was to persuade one of those with knowledge of the apartment to talk about its security, access and escape routes. 'And as you know,' as Harper said to Maggie May, 'I can be very persuasive.'

Operating from the cover of empty buildings or street-front bars and cafes, Harper, Maggie May and Barry Big staked out the roads leading to the apartment and tracked the Thais whenever they left the building. Either Narong or Decha was always on duty at the apartment along with two of the other soldiers, while the other three took time off. On the first three nights, the three off-duty men kept together, drinking and eating in heavily populated areas where it would have been difficult to isolate and abduct them, before heading back to the army compound where they were based. However on the fourth night, Decha remained in a go-go bar and brothel in a side-street while the other two disappeared.

Two hours later, Decha, by now quite drunk, came out of the brothel and began walking up the street towards the main road. He had gone only a few yards when Harper stepped out of an alleyway, side-swiped him across the throat, and as the Thai gasped frantically for breath, Harper hit him with a savage punch that snapped his head around. As Decha dropped to the ground, Maggie May pulled to a halt in a rusting Toyota pick-up truck. Harper dumped the unconscious Thai into the back and they roared off up the street.

When Decha came around, coughing and spluttering as a bucket of water was dumped over him, he found himself immobile, lashed by cable ties to a chair in the windowless basement of the safe house, and with Harper standing over him. He pulled up his sleeve and showed the Thai the track marks on his arms. 'This is what you did to me,' he said. 'If you don't tell me what I need to know, then I'll kill you without a second thought.'

'Do it then,' Decha said. 'I'm not telling you anything.' His voice did not sound anywhere as sure as his words suggested, but he cleared his throat and spat noisily at Harper. The spit flecked across Harper's trousers.

Harper pulled out his combat knife and showed it to the Thai, whose eyes followed the blade as Harper moved it to and fro in front of him. 'I need you to tell me everything you know about the apartment where you're repackaging the heroin,' Harper said. 'What the security systems are, how many people are there - both the people doing the packaging and the ones watching over them -any codes or passwords you use and how you would get away if there's a police raid or a fire. Ready to talk?'

The Thai remained silent, his face set like stone.

'No?' Harper said. 'Big mistake. Now I don't know if you've watched many gangster movies, but when they do this in films, they always seem to start with the little finger and work their way up. However, I'm a man in a hurry, so we're going to go a different route. Do you know what distinguishes us from the apes?'

Decha stared at him, fear in his eyes, the sweat of panic on his brow. 'I- I don't know.'

'Well, you clearly weren't paying enough attention in school, were you? The answer is opposable thumbs.'

He pinned the Thai's right thumb under the blade, then severed it with a blow from the heel of his hand on the back of the knife. There was an unearthly scream but Harper blotted it out. The man was meat, not human, and meat didn't feel pain.

'Ready to talk yet?' Harper said, moving the knife to the other thumb. 'No?' There was another blood-curdling scream as Harper hacked it off.

'Then I guess there's nothing to distinguish you from an ape now, is there? By the way, when I've finished with your fingers, your tongue and your cock are next, that's if you don't bleed to death first.' He tossed the bloody stump onto the floor. As he raised the knife again, Decha cried 'Stop! Stop! I'll tell you everything you want to know.' The man began to sob uncontrollably.

Harper made him go over every detail of the access to the building, the security systems, the number of people working there and where they sat or stood, right down to the location of the toilet, and what the escape plan would be if there was a raid. When he had finished interrogating him, the Thai gave him a fearful look. 'What happens now?'

Harper shrugged, his expression set like stone. 'What you'd expect. You left me for dead, now it's your turn.'

As the Thai soldier unleashed a torrent of curses in his native dialect, Harper forced Decha's chin back, then slit his throat with one stroke of his knife and watched impassive as the life-blood pumped from him. When he heard the death-rattle in the Thai's throat, he wiped the blade of his knife on Decha's sleeve and walked out. The rent was paid for three months. There were no neighbours to complain about the smell and the fresh rat droppings in the cellar suggested that by the time the owner came to investigate, Harper would be long gone and the dead Thai mere bones.

Harper brought Barry Big, Maggie May and Hansfree up to speed and then laid out his plan. 'As you know, the factory is on the top floor and the security is close to impregnable. But if there's a raid, their plan is to escape over the roof tops and down through a neighbouring building while the cops are still fighting their way up the stairs. That's the weak point.'

For his plan to be effective, Harper needed a couple of smoke grenades. Bangkok was a city were almost everything imaginable could be purchased at a price and smoke canisters, pinched from the police or army or sold off from their armouries by junior ranks boosting their modest incomes, were kept under the counter of a number of stalls in the city's teeming markets. However Harper preferred to improvise what he needed using fireworks that were even more widely available. He bought half a dozen large "Starburst" fireworks and, using only wooden tools, since any spark from a metal tool could have caused a fatal explosion, he carefully removed the fuses from each one and emptied out the contents. He now had a mound of coarse-grained black powder and two handfuls of the marble-sized explosive pellets that were hurled into the sky when the firework ignited to create the starburst.

He took two empty plastic bottles - one should have been enough but for the plan to be failsafe he needed a spare in case one failed to detonate - and filled them with the black powder and the explosive pellets. He tamped the powder down carefully with a piece of scrap wood and then fitted one of the fuses he had removed from the fireworks to either end of the bottle. When he had finished, he was holding two improvised devices like the "flash-bang" stun grenades used by special forces, but without the accompanying gas. The fuses could be lit by a cigarette end and once detonated in a confined space like the stairwell of the apartment building where the heroin was re-packaged, the home-made flash-bangs would create a deafening, disorientating noise, accompanied by dense clouds of smoke that would billow up through the building on the updraft. He handed them to Barry Big and then ran through the plan and the timings with him one last time.

While Barry Big stationed himself within range of the entrance to the apartment block, Harper broke into an empty building further down the street. He went up the stairs to the top floor, climbed out of a roof-light and then made his way across the rooftops until he found a hiding place behind a rusting steel vent, a few yards from the skylights in the apartment. He settled himself there and then made a final check of his untraceable Colt 45. It was old and well-used but still in good condition.

Harper slid off the safety catch and then gave a double-click on the communication device at his wrist, a Japanese throw-away walkie talkie. There was an answering click and a moment later he heard two short bursts of fire as Barry Big took out the two guards in the entrance to the building. There was a heartbeat's silence, and then a double Crump! sound as he detonated the improvised smoke canisters in the stairwell. There was no need to attempt to breach the steel grilles, doors and shutters, nor run the gauntlet of armed guards on each landing, because when dense smoke started billowing up through the building, Narong, the other two soldiers and a Thai in civilian clothes who must have been part of the gang, all headed for the roof.

Harper was waiting for them. He held his fire until they had all clambered out onto the roof, then picked them off, double-tapping each of them, switching to the next target even as the previous one was still falling to the roof-tiles, their heads haloed by a spray of blood and brains. Harper's controlled fire came so fast that the double-taps seemed to merge into one continuous burst of firing. The last to die was Narong. Harper gut-shot him, determined that his death would be a slow one. As the Thai's pistol slid from his grasp and skittered away across the tiles, Harper emerged from the cover of the steel vent and Narong's eyes widened in recognition and fear when he saw him.

'You should have gone with your instincts and killed me in the opium fields, while you had the chance,' Harper said. 'Now it's your turn and it's going to be slow.' He levelled his Colt and put a second round into Narong's kidneys and another into his lung.

He picked up Narong's pistol and was about to walk away when he heard women's voices crying in terror. He glanced around, stepped to the edge of the roof and looked down into the street. It remained quiet for now - prudent neighbours in such districts did not go looking for trouble, least of all when gunfire had been heard - and there was no sign of any police response as yet.

He crossed the roof to the skylight and looked down into the apartment. Smoke was still billowing though the room below, which was now deserted except for six women, all stark naked apart from white surgical masks covering their noses and mouths. They were chained by their ankles with padlocks fixed to the steel tables on which they had been repacking the heroin.

Drums of the uncut heroin stood open next to the table, with plastic packs of the finished and repackaged end product stacked against the wall. Bundles of American dollars - it was hard to estimate how much but perhaps $50,000 in all - were piled on a table at the far end of the room. The six chained women were screaming in terror and making frantic attempts to break their chains. Harper had to shout several times to silence them and get their attention. 'Do any of you speak English?'

One of them nodded, a frighteningly young-looking Thai girl with tear tracks through the white dust on her cheeks.

'Right. Tell the others to stop screaming. They don't need to be afraid, because the smoke is not from a fire, it's just a smoke grenade. The men who were here are all dead, so you've nothing more to fear from them. Who had the keys to your padlocks?'

'Narong had them.'

'Wait, I'll be back in a moment,' Harper said and turned away, ignoring the girls' redoubled cries.

He retraced his steps across the roof to where Narong lay. He already looked close to death, but Harper kept the barrel of his rifle pressed into the Thai's neck while he searched his pockets with the other hand and found the keys. He walked back across the roof, climbed down the ladder propped against the edge of the skylight. He unchained the girl he had spoken to, then gave her the keys. 'Undo the locks and release the others,' he said. 'Now is there anybody else here or were you the only ones?'

She gestured towards a door in the far wall. 'I think there are some boys in there. I've never seen them - Narong always kept the door locked - but I've heard them crying out.'

'All right, I'll take a look but don't wait, you all need to get out of here now. Don't try to use the stairs, there may still be guards there. Climb out of the skylight, go across the roof and down through the other building. I've left the roof light to it open; that's your escape route and your chance for a new life. Take all the dollars you can carry, share them between you and then get right away from here and don't ever come back.'

However, even as he said it, he saw the dead eyes and hollow faces of the other women, suggesting that they were all already hooked on smack and unlikely to break free. Narong and the men who had been running the place were dead or as good as dead, but others would soon take their places and business as usual would no doubt resume. He waited until the girl had begun to climb the ladder and then hurried to the door she had indicated. He didn't bother to find the right key, two savage kicks with his boot splintered the frame and the door flew open.

Harper barrelled into the room, the pistol tracking his gaze as he dived and rolled and came up ready to fire, but there were no guards, just two Arab-looking teenage boys. Their legs were shackled, their wrists chained to the wall, and the expensive clothes they were wearing were stained, torn and covered in filth. Both looked semi-comatose and a quick body search of them revealed track marks on their arms and legs that Harper was only too familiar with on his own body.

'It's all right,' Harper said. 'You're safe now'. One of them was still out of it, head lolling, but the other muttered a reply.

After struggling with the chains pinning them to the wall for a few moments, he drew his pistol and put a couple of rounds though one of the links before he could set them free. He then picked up the comatose boy in a fireman's lift and carried him up to the roof, before returning for the other one.

'Are you British?' the boy said as Harper helped him to his feet. His voice was still drowsy but his English was impeccable.

Harper smiled. 'I might be, but the important thing from your point of view is that I'm not Thai.'

'Please help us,' the boy said.

'I already have,' Harper said. 'I've killed the men who were holding you here and undone your chains. You just need to get out of here now. Can you stand? Okay, come on then, I'll show you the way.'

The boy was so weak and emaciated that Harper had to help him up the ladder and onto the roof. The boy saw Narong lying in a pool of his own blood. He walked over to him, spat in his face and cursed him in Arabic and English. He drew back his foot to kick Narong, but Harper grabbed his arm. 'Believe me, I sympathise with your feelings,' he said, 'but we need to move fast now. Police and maybe some other people we wouldn't want to meet will be arriving soon.'

The other boy was now able to get to his feet but both were so unsteady that Harper had to help them down through the roof light he'd used to access the roof from the empty building, and then guide them down the stairs. He held up a hand, motioning them to silence while he eased open the outside door and checked up and down the street. There were no signs of trouble. He thumbed the button on his walkie-talkie as they emerged onto the street. 'BB,' he said, 'I need a hand; I've got company.'

Barry Big's rasping voice cut through the static on the walkie-talkie. 'I can see that,' he said. 'I'm watching you. What gives with them?'

'Another couple of Narong's victims. I'm just giving them a helping hand.'

'Gathering waifs and strays, Lex,' Maggie May chipped in. 'That's not your usual style at all. They're not exactly fast-moving are they?'

'Nor would you be if you'd been chained to a wall for a few weeks. It's fine, but they're too weak to make it on their own, so BB, you'll need to help me. Maggie May, you watch our backs till we're out of the immediate area and then RV with us at the safe house, in fifteen.'

'Roger that,' she said.

'Hansfree? Any police or army chatter yet?'

Monitoring communications back at the safe house, Hansfree was close to the limit of the walkie-talkie's range and his voice came up faintly through a fog of static. 'Just really getting started,' he said. 'A flurry in the last couple minutes, so they're on their way. If you're not already, you need to be out of there sharpish.'

'On the move now,' Harper said and broke the connection just as Barry Big appeared. He took the weaker of the two Arab boys, draping the boy's arm over his shoulder and putting his own powerful arm around his waist, while Harper helped the other one along.

They had only gone about fifty yards when they heard the first police sirens in the distance.

'All right,' Harper said. 'We need to move as fast as you can go.' As the sound of sirens grew louder, they ducked down a side street and then hurried along the parallel road. The boys were close to exhaustion and when they reached the junction with a busy through road, Harper shot another glance at them, then flagged down a cab. 'Really?' Barry Big said, giving him a questioning look.

'It's a risk, but a lesser one than staying on the streets and moving at this pace,' Harper said. 'But in case we're compromised, we'll need to be clear of the safe house in double-quick time.'

'Don't say anything while we're in the taxi,' he said to the boys, before they climbed in. He gave the cab-driver directions to a street corner fifty yards from the safe house and tipped him big as he dropped them off. As Harper had indicated to Barry Big, using a taxi to drop them almost within sight of a safe house was not a risk he would normally have taken, but the boys were all in, and even if the cab-driver did shop them to the cops, they would have abandoned the safe house before a police follow-up could get there.

They RV'd with Hansfree at the safe house, and Maggie May arrived a couple of minutes later. Harper gave them a quick summary of what had happened up on the roof. 'I got the Thais, so that's done,' he said. 'And if I'd had any reservations about killing them what I saw in the apartment would have answered them. Apart from these boys, there were thousands of dollars in bundles and enough heroin to feed ten thousand drug habits, but there were six naked women too. The dealers were using them as slave labour to cut the drugs and re-pack them for sale.'

'Naked?' Maggie May said, shuddering. 'For sex?'

'No, although from what I saw of Narong and his men, I wouldn't rule that out either, but mainly so they couldn't hide heroin or cash in their clothing. They were worth less than dogs to Narong and his crew. When they tried to escape, thinking the building was on fire, the women were still chained to the steel table where they were packing the drugs. So they left these boys and those women there to die. I can't get one of them out of my mind. She was so young, little more than a child, and yet the look in her eyes was that of an old woman.' He shivered at the memory. 'Okay, let's pack up, sanitise the place fast and get out of here. If the cab driver who dropped us grasses us and the Thai cops do a sweep, we'll already be gone but I don't want them to find anything that could link back to us. When we're done here, travel separately as usual and take different flights out of the country. The normal payments will be nestling in your bank accounts by the time you get home.'

'What about your new best friends?' Maggie May said.

He shrugged. 'I'll take them to a hotel while I work out the best way to get them to safety. One thing's for sure, they can't stay here and nor can we. Let's move it.'

Hansfree loaded his specialist comms kit into his hired car and made straight for the airport. Harper also left with the boys at once, leaving Maggie May and Barry Big to finish sanitising the safe house, wiping down any surface that might have been touched with an ungloved hand and bagging all their rubbish, before dumping it a safe distance away on their way to the airport.

Fearing the boys might collapse from hunger, thirst and exhaustion, Harper made them drink some water and bought them some street food from a stall a few hundred yards away from the safe house. The weaker boy barely swallowed a mouthful of chicken and rice before shaking his head and pushing it away, but the other one devoured his in a few bites. Harper then took them to a dingy hotel where the owner pocketed the cash he proffered and did not even raise an eyebrow at the sight of an Englishman disappearing into a room with two young boys who were clearly not his sons.

The room was filthy and the sheets clearly hadn't been changed since the previous occupant had left, but he wasn't planning a long stay, so it suited him well enough. 'Right,' he said, as soon as he had closed the door. 'Tell me everything about how you got into this situation and then we'll work out how to get you safely out of it.' He focussed on the stronger of the two boys, since the other one had now gone semi-comatose again. 'My name's Lex. What's yours?'

'I am Faisal bin Muqrin.'

'Where are you from, Faisal?'

'Saudi Arabia,' he said nervously. He reached into his pocket and took out a Saudi Arabian ID card.

Harper took the card and examined it. 'From the way you speak English, I'd say you'd been educated at an English school?'

Faisal nodded. 'Yes, in England. Near Leeds. My friend and I had just finished our A-levels,' Faisal said, 'and we'd come to Thailand for a holiday as a treat, but we got separated from our bodyguards in the Khlong Toei red light district.'

'Your parents didn't come with you?'

'They stay in Saudi Arabia. They do not like to leave the Kingdom.'

'I'm guessing you got separated from your bodyguards on purpose,' Harper said, with a smile. 'Perhaps you were anxious to sample a little of what Thailand has to offer, without word getting back to your parents - maybe hoping to lose your virginity to a bar girl or try out a Thai lady boy? But then you got more than you bargained for, didn't you?'

The boy hung his head. 'The man called Narong stopped us in the street.,' he said, his voice barely above a whisper. 'He was wearing military uniform and had two other soldiers with him. He told us that a bar girl had been raped by two young men answering our description.'

'That's not something the army would normally get involved in,' Harper said.

'We didn't know that. When he told us to hand over our passports and said we were under arrest, we just thought it was a misunderstanding and we'd be released as soon as they realised their mistake.'

'They were probably just going to shake you down for whatever money and valuables you had,' Harper said, 'but then you and your friend made the mistake of mentioning who your fathers were, right?'

The boy nodded. 'They took us to the place where you found us and locked us up. Another man came then, also in uniform. The others called him Colonel, and deferred to him. He interrogated us and began trying to blackmail our fathers.'

'How do you know that?'

'He made us hold up a copy of that day's newspaper, and filmed us. He made us say that if a ransom wasn't paid, we'd be killed.'

'And was it? Did your families pay?'

'I don't know, but it was him who told Narong to inject us with heroin.'

While they were talking, the boy was looking increasingly strung out, scratching furiously at his skin and switching his gaze from side to side as if a supply of heroin might have been stashed under the bed. 'Try and take it easy,' Harper said, not unkindly. 'I'm going to get you to a place where you'll be safe and where they can start to give you the help you need, and see about getting you home.'

Using his burner phone, he made contact with Hansfree, who was at the airport waiting for his flight to be called. 'Hansfree, I need the numbers of a private ambulance company and a drug rehabilitation clinic, the more discreet and exclusive the better. Can you do that?'

'Give me five minutes,' Hansfree said and broke the connection.

He was quicker than that. Within three minutes at the most the burner phone pinged and Harper found a text with two numbers. However, when he phoned the clinic, they told him they were fully booked, and even though he assured them that money - US dollars - was no object, they proved immovable. 'Brilliant,' he said, shaking his head. 'I've managed to find the only business in Thailand that can't be bribed with a pile of dollars.'

'What do we do now?' the Saudi boy said.

Harper thought for a few more moments. 'We go to Plan B,' he said. 'It's slightly more risky, but it will also get you home quicker. The best thing is to get you to the Saudi embassy but we'll not ring to give them advance warning because if the phones are being tapped - and in Thailand that's a strong possibility - and your captors had friends in high places, as I'm sure they did, there might be an attempt to recapture you, or even kill you. Don't worry,' he said as he saw the alarm flare in the boy's eyes. 'I'm here to make sure that doesn't happen, but we need to approach it with care, just in case.'

Leaving the boys in the hotel room with a burner phone they could use to contact Harper in an emergency and strict instructions not to open the door to anyone but him, he hurried over to a nearby shopping mall. He returned after half an hour with some truly hideous American-style clothes for the boys: trainers, loud check Bermuda shorts, US college polo shirts with frat house insignia, New York Yankees baseball caps and pairs of wraparound dark glasses. He also had an equally tasteless outfit for himself.

'Put these on, 'Harper said. 'They're horrible I know and you don't look American on a close inspection, but to a casual glance, we'll all pass as Yank tourists.'

'Why do we have to look like Americans?'

'Because the USA is Thailand's most powerful ally and the Thai military and their intelligence agencies will be more reluctant to risk an incident by manhandling American citizens than they would be for most other countries, including Saudi Arabia.'

Harper's team had now already left the country, but he knew a couple of local heavies that he could use as back-up. They operated on the margins of the Bangkok underworld and had ridden shotgun on some of his shadier activities in the past. They turned up within an hour in answer to his summons, and walked flanking the boys when they set off, while Harper carried out counter-surveillance, making sure they were not being watched or followed. When they got closer to the Saudi embassy in Bangkok's glitzy Bang Rak district in a bend of the Chao Phraya river, he left the boys and their minders in a coffee shop while he went ahead to scout out the entrance to the embassy.

Harper had already weighed up the pros and cons of approaching the building. All embassies tended to be under surveillance by agents of different intelligence agencies, domestic and foreign, friendly and hostile, and there was no reason to believe the Saudi one would be an exception. For a man who lived his life under the radar as much as Harper, being seen or filmed entering or leaving any embassy could be problematic, but the Thais and the Saudis were both long-term British allies, and there was no reason why a former British soldier and now a freelance security expert - which was as much as the outside world knew about Harper's unusual line of work - should not be consulted on security matters.

He spent an hour observing the embassy, scrutinising the people loitering around it and those entering or leaving, before deciding it would be safe to approach the guard at the embassy gate. By-passing the long line of Thais waiting patiently to apply for Saudi work permits, he handed Faisal's ID card to a security guard and said 'Take this to the HOC - the Head of Chancery - at once.'

The guard was not used to being ordered about by visitors to the embassy, but something about Harper's tone and bearing persuaded him that it would be wise to comply and he disappeared into the embassy. He returned almost immediately and ushered Harper through the security scanner and took him to an interview room deep inside the embassy.

An immaculately, very expensively-dressed man was waiting there, flanked by two armed guards. The HOC was in his early thirties and very intense-looking, with the corners of his mouth permanently downturned, as if in distaste, Harper thought, at some of the people he had to deal with and the things he had to do in service of his nation. The man wasted no time on pleasantries. 'I demand to know how and where you obtained that card,' he said, speaking in flawless, accentless English, 'and where its owner can be found. I must warn you that if this is an attempt at more blackmail' - Lex raised an eye at the word 'more' but made no comment - 'then you are in the worst place in Thailand to try it. You are now standing in the Sovereign Territory of the Kingdom of Saudi Arabia and here the laws and customs of Saudi Arabia are in force. For stealing we can sever the left hand, for murder we can sever your head with a sword and for attempted blackmail the punishment is somewhere in between.'

Lex spent a moment trying to picture which part of the anatomy the Saudis might think was appropriate for a blackmail case, then gave up and handed the HOC the second ID card. 'These two young men are nearby,' he said, 'but they need urgent help. I found and rescued them and will hand them over to your safekeeping, and for those efforts I neither expect nor want anything. They happened to have been captured by men with whom I have an ongoing vendetta, some of whom are no longer in a position to do them any further harm. However, there are powerful men who will have been angered by the losses they've suffered and who would certainly wish the boys harm if they should fall into their hands. I believe they may be at risk until they are safely inside the embassy. I will be happy to answer any further questions then, as will they - as far as they are able, because as part of their ordeal, both of them have repeatedly been injected with heroin. However, I rely on you to ensure there are no delays when we get here.'

'I will arrange a team of our people to escort you.'

Harper shook his head. 'I thank you for that offer, but that will merely draw attention to us and the sort of men we are dealing with won't be deterred by mere manpower.'

The HOC hesitated for a moment but then gave him the assurances that he was seeking. 'You and the boys will be admitted to the embassy immediately, but you will then be held in a secure area until their identities have been confirmed and your stories have been verified.'

'As you wish,' Harper said, 'though I must again stress that what these boys need most of is urgent medical attention, so I hope delays will be kept to a minimum.'

He was shown out and, having made the usual series of counter-surveillance manoeuvres to make sure he was not being followed, he went to collect the boys. Both of them now looked very shaky, deep in the grip of heroin withdrawal - a feeling he knew only too well himself - but he eyeballed each of them in turn, telling them 'If you keep your heads together now, within ten minutes you'll be safe inside the embassy and whatever you need will be provided. Don't let me down now.'

Still in their garish American style clothes and flanked by the two burly Thai minders, they walked slowly towards the embassy while Harper once more ran counter-surveillance. When he saw Harper approaching, the guard at the gate - obviously now well-briefed - stepped aside and waved them through. As soon as they were inside the embassy, Harper nodded to the two Thai minders, who melted away back into the crowds around the gates. He began to relax as he and the boys passed through the marble lobby and were steered into the room where the HOC was waiting,

He had greeted Harper without warmth before, but his attitude now changed completely. He shook him by the hand, then turned to the boys, and having checked that their faces matched the photographs on the ID cards, he broke into a broad grin. Ignoring their ridiculous clothes and filthy condition, he embraced them both, pouring out a flood of Arabic and praising Allah for their safe deliverance. Abandoning any thought of further security screening, he immediately ushered the boys and Harper through from the anteroom to a lavishly furnished receiving room, where servants were waiting with mint tea and fresh dates, but the boys were so deep in withdrawal they barely took in their surroundings.

'They need urgent medical help,' Harper said to the HOC. He nodded and hurried out of the room but when he returned a few moments later it was not with a medic but the ambassador, a tall, overweight figure with a hooked nose and a carefully manicured goatee. The headdress of his flowing white robe was banded with gold, which Harper knew was a sign of high birth.

The ambassador took the boys' hands, also praised Allah for their safe return from danger, and then told them they would be able to speak to their fathers by phone very shortly, but the news that their sons had been found had already been communicated to them.

He then turned to Harper. 'And what is your role in this, Mr… I'm sorry, I don't believe I've been told your name?'

'Just call me Lex, Mr Ambassador,' Harper said, 'but please get some medical help for these boys straight away. They have been through a lot and their troubles are not yet over.' He pulled up the sleeve of Faisal's jacket to reveal the track marks on his arm.

The ambassador's face darkened, but he picked up a phone at once and barked a series of orders into it. Within moments a couple of embassy underlings ran into the room and began to lead the boys away. Faisal pulled away from them, grabbed Harper's arm and began to pour out his thanks, but Harper held up a hand to stem the flow and just said, 'No thanks needed. Just get yourselves well again.' He thought about giving the boys a hug, but decided protocol required something more formal, so he shook their hands instead.

Left alone with the ambassador and the HOC, Harper answered a few of their questions and explained some, but only some, of the circumstances by which he'd come to find the boys. When he'd finished, the ambassador fell silent for a moment but then gathered himself, and extended his hand. 'Not only the boys' fathers, but the whole kingdom owe you a debt of gratitude,' he said. 'How may we contact you, so that we may express our thanks in a suitable way?'

'As I've already told your HOC, I didn't do this for a reward,' Harper said. 'I gave our young friends a contact number for me, though I do change my number fairly frequently.'

The ambassador gave an enigmatic smile. 'Then we must make sure to use it swiftly. And what kind of work brought you to Thailand?'

Harper returned the smile. 'I'm ex-military, now working in the security field.'

'An answer that explains everything and nothing,' the ambassador said, still with the same smile. 'But your business is your own affair of course, and I'm just grateful that, thanks to you, the young princes will be restored safely to their families. Insh'Allah, all will be well with them from now on.'

'They were princes?' asked Harper. 'They didn't tell me that.'

'Their fathers teach them at a young age to conceal their royal heritage while overseas. It is safer that way.'

'Was any ransom paid?' asked Harper.

The ambassador's smile snapped off like a light. 'That is not something I can discuss.' He paused, gathering his thoughts and when he spoke again, the diplomatic smile was back in place. 'You understand of course, that such matters are highly confidential. Were it to become known that the Saudi government was willing to pay substantial ransoms for the return of our kidnapped nationals, the number of kidnappings would increase dramatically, I think.'

'I understand completely,' Harper said.

The ambassador gave him a thoughtful look. 'Tell me, Lex, are you familiar with the Saudi custom of Honour and Dishonour? Under our customs, bad deeds can lead to blood feuds lasting for generations but by the same token, doing a special favour for a Saudi can lead to a lifelong alliance in which "Your enemy is my enemy; your friend is my friend". We now have a debt of honour to you and rest assured it will be repaid in full.' He glanced at his watch. 'Alas, I have important business that will wait no longer. Thank you my friend, your service to the kingdom will not be forgotten.'

The HOC showed Harper out, but he paused as they reached the entrance gates. 'Let me make some enquiries, Lex, and then, if you are willing, we may perhaps speak again about a matter of mutual interest.'

Harper smiled. 'You may find me a little elusive.'

'And you may find that we can be very thorough and very persistent. The expatriate community in Thailand is a small one, and if we wish to find you, rest assured, we will do so. We are a wealthy nation, and wealth can buy knowledge, and knowledge is power. But if we should send for you, it will be because we believe we can do good things together, to your benefit as well as ours.'

Chapter 6

Harper returned to Pattaya and was walking along the beach road a couple of mornings later, on the way to his favourite coffee shop, when he became aware of a Thai man standing on the pavement ahead of him, looking in his direction. He was dressed in civilian clothes, but something about his bearing told Harper that he was police or military. Harper slowed his pace a fraction, raised an arm as if waving to a car passing in the opposite direction and used that as cover to glance behind him. Another heavy-set Thai twenty yards behind him slowed his own pace too, pretending to study a window display, and just behind him yet another man put his foot on a bench and began re-tying a shoelace that was not undone.

Harper felt the adrenaline surge as he went into fight or flight mode. The path of least resistance lay ahead. He could flatten the man staring at him, lose the two who were following him and circle back to his apartment to grab his bug-out bag. If his place was also being watched, then he had enough in the hip-pack he wore, including his fake Irish passport, to get out of the country either through the airport or, more likely if he was under such intense surveillance, across the border into Cambodia or Laos, or across the Kra Isthmus and down the peninsula to Malaysia.

While Harper was processing this, as if reading his mind, the man ahead of him spread his hands in a friendly gesture, smiled and called out 'Please do not be alarmed. I merely wish to give you an invitation from my employer. He would be honoured if you would join him for lunch tomorrow at this Japanese restaurant in Bangkok.' Still on maximum alert, Harper walked slowly forwards and took the card that the man was holding out to him.

'And your employer is?'

The man smiled. 'All will be revealed at the restaurant. My employer said one o'clock tomorrow.' He turned and walked away and when Harper glanced behind him, he saw that the two men tailing him were also heading away back up the street.

For a few moments he hesitated, assessing his options. It was possible he was being lured into a trap, but if so, why choose a public place like a restaurant rather than somewhere more discreet? And in any case, had the mysterious figures genuinely wished him harm, there had been ample opportunity here in the street to shoot him or overpower him by sheer weight of numbers. The summons, couched in the polite terms of an invitation, was both puzzling and more than a little alarming, but Harper's curiosity was also piqued.

The following morning, he made the ninety minute drive from Pattaya to Bangkok and reached the street where the restaurant was sited two hours before the specified time. He found a cafe and took a seat at a window table where he could observe the front of the restaurant, then sat there sipping black coffee and watching and waiting. He could detect no sign that anyone else had the building under surveillance and, other than a few tourists and Thai businessmen taking an early lunch, there appeared to be no significant traffic in or out of the restaurant until just before one o'clock, when a limousine with military pennants on its wings pulled up outside. A uniformed soldier, acting as chauffeur, jumped out and held the passenger door open and Harper caught a brief glimpse of a tall, dark haired figure dressed in the uniform of a Colonel in the Thai Airborne Forces, striding across the pavement and disappearing inside the restaurant.

Harper took his time, finishing his coffee and paying his bill before walking across the street and into the restaurant. Although he did not give his name, the maitre d' appeared to know exactly who he was and at once led him up the stairs to a private room on the first floor. Harper's host, the man he had seen earlier, rose to greet him. 'Thank you for joining me at such short notice,' he said. 'My name is Colonel Channarong. I've been hoping for an opportunity to meet you for a while and now, here we are.' He gave a broad smile. He looked to be in his early forties, with jet-black hair and a charming, urbane manner that did not distract Harper from noting the shrewdness of the other man's penetrating gaze. He made small talk about the weather and the latest political crisis in fluent English and when Harper complimented him on his language skills, the Thai smiled again. 'I acquired them at considerable expense to my parents, at a public school in the UK.'

He then summoned a waiter and ordered lunch for both of them. 'I know this restaurant well. You will allow me to order for both of us?' It was as much a statement as a question.

Harper shrugged. 'Why not?' He was wondering to himself how long the game of cat and mouse would continue before Channarong came to the point. He had his answer after they had both been served with a glass of sake. The colonel put the tips of his fingers together as he studied Harper across the table. 'You have lived here for some time, Mr Harper - as you see, I know your real name.' He could not hide a slightly self-satisfied smile as he said it. 'I have many sources of information, both official and unofficial, and very little happens here that does not come to my attention sooner or later. I could tell you things that would make even your hair stand on end. There are wealthy Europeans, most of them British, of course, given your countrymen's traditional appetite for such things, whose liking for sex with very young boys would end their careers in an instant and probably lead to imprisonment if it were ever to be revealed.

There are Middle Eastern princelings with a taste for equally unusual and extreme forms of sexual gratification, and many others who think they have found a safe haven here: money launderers, swindlers and con men, thieves and even murderers…'

'Don't forget blackmailers,' Said Harper, interrupting the man's flow.

The colonel raised an eyebrow but continued speaking. 'We are, how would you put it? A broad church? And we can accommodate all sorts of people.'

'Just as long as they're able to make their pay-offs.'

'I would have preferred a more elegant way of putting it, Mr Harper,' Channarong said, 'but yes, their welcome comes at a price. They must make a contribution to the cost of their freedom to enjoy their pastimes, though it is probably much less than the taxes they are evading in their home countries.' He paused, giving Harper a calculating look. 'Now I'm not sure if you fully understand how things work here. We in the military have found it necessary to replace the civilian government from time to time but even when a civilian government is in office, do not ever be in any doubt about where the real power lies in this country.'

His voice was now cold and the look he directed at Harper was even more glacial. 'For myself, I'm very well connected to our friends in the US special forces and military intelligence, and in the past my military career has taken me into Cambodia, Laos and Vietnam.' Again there was the bleak smile, 'albeit in an unofficial capacity, shall we say.'

Harper kept his expression neutral as he studied the Thai colonel. Despite his urbane manner, he looked like a man who would kill you without a second thought if you tried to double-cross him, or cut your hand off with a knife if he happened to take a fancy to your signet ring.

'So, to the business of this meeting,' Channarong said, dabbing the corner of his mouth with his napkin. 'No one enters and leaves this country with the regularity with which you have done, without coming to our attention. Nor, despite the warm welcome we offer to foreign investors, can someone with no company directorships or other visible sources of income, pass such substantial sums of money through his various bank accounts, here, in Singapore, and, no doubt, many other offshore jurisdictions, without attracting our interest.' He paused. 'So we not only know who you are, we know what you are involved in. And not everyone here is as fond of the British as I am. Now you may have heard that we lost several members of our special forces recently?'

Harper felt his pulse begin to accelerate, but kept his expression neutral. 'I'm sorry to hear that but it's the risk that every soldier runs.'

The colonel's cold smile did not alter. 'That's true, of course, but these men were not killed in action. They were executed right here in Bangkok. It could have been a gangland killing, but that doesn't really add up.'

'Really? Why is that?'

'Because although they were involved with narcotics, anyone on the street would have known that these particular men had some very high level protection. And whoever killed them didn't touch the heroin - and there was well over a million dollars worth of that - lying in plain view at the apartment where they were shot. Some dollars had been taken, but I suspect they were stolen by the women who had been mixing and packing the heroin. Again, that was a rather quixotic gesture and most unlike the actions of any gangster I've ever met. In fact it was more the sort of act one might expect from an English gentleman.'

Harper kept his gaze steady. 'And if you've done your research on me Colonel, you'll know that while I may be English, I'm definitely not a fucking gentleman.'

'Indeed so,' Channarong said, 'but it remains a puzzle nonetheless. All the more so, because there has been no attempt to move in on the heroin operation, which if it had been a gangland killing, would certainly have happened by now. And there's one more strange thing: the method of killing did not have the hallmarks of a gangland execution either. This was not a drive-by shooting, cutting them down in a hail of bullets. It was meticulously planned and executed, taking advantage of the one flaw in the apartment's very effective security arrangements.' His gaze again flickered to Harper's face.

'Well that's certainly puzzling, but why are you telling me all this?'

'Because I was wondering if you could shed any light on it,' he said. 'You weren't involved by any chance, were you - directly or indirectly?'

'Of course not.' Harper's mind was racing but he kept his voice steady. 'Why would you think that I was?'

The colonel's smile grew even more frozen. 'Because those men were known to you. They were part of your escort on a recent operation you undertook into Myanmar. Yes, Mr Harper, I also know about that.'

Harper shrugged. 'Then you'll also know that my escort abandoned me in Myanmar, leaving me to make my own way back across the border.'

'Indeed so, which is precisely why you might have wanted to take revenge.'

Harper shrugged. 'If I tried to take revenge on everyone who had let me down, Colonel, I'd never have time to do anything else. Now, I'm sorry to hear about your men, but I had nothing to do with that.'

There was a long silence. Channarong lit a cigarette and blew a stream of smoke towards the ceiling before again fixing Harper with his gaze. 'The fate of those men is not an overriding concern for me personally - they were disposable and easily replaceable - but they were working for a very senior Thai general and, to put it mildly, he is not well pleased at the disruption to the income stream that funds his rather extravagant lifestyle. He's already had us turning Bangkok upside down, shaking down every informer and street criminal, and he won't rest until he finds the person or persons responsible and has them killed.' He paused again. 'As I said, whether those men lived or died was a matter of indifference to me, but the perpetrator also gave me personal cause for annoyance by removing two young men who were staying in the apartment as my guests, while a suitable method for reuniting them with their families was being discussed.'

'That sounds awfully like kidnapping, Colonel,' Harper said, leaning back in his chair with a nonchalance he didn't altogether feel, 'but I'm still not sure how any of this affects me.'

'Because unless you have some, how can I put it - logistical assistance here - sooner or later you may find yourself arrested, or you may be killed. This is not a land the puts much stock in British notions of justice, Mr Harper, like innocent until proven guilty. Where the general is concerned, there is no requirement for due process of law, proof of guilt beyond reasonable doubt, or even any evidence. Mere suspicion is enough and the sentence is always summary execution. So I am offering to provide you with the logistical assistance you will need, including providing the general with a suitable scapegoat for the killing of his men.'

Harper studied him for a moment. 'So what are you looking for in return, Colonel?' he asked eventually. 'I don't expect that you are offering this from the kindness of your heart.'

Channarong inclined his head. 'In return, you will need to increase the already substantial fees for your various activities by a further forty per cent.' He studied Harper's expression as he waited for a response. 'What can I say Mr Harper? It's the way of the modern world and I'm sure those with whom you do business will understand. After all, it seems that everything is subject to inflation these days.'

'And I shall pass that additional forty per cent on to you, of course. I thank you for your generous offer, Colonel, and I shall give it every consideration. Of course, there would be nothing to stop me from agreeing to your terms and then leaving the country and never coming back, would there?'

Channarong smiled. 'Nothing at all, except that you clearly enjoy living in the Land Of Smiles and under my protection you will enjoy even greater freedom, security and opportunities too, that would not be open to you elsewhere. And even if you do flee Thailand, you would be wise not to underestimate our reach; we have friends in many other places around the world.'

He allowed the silence to grow for a few seconds before speaking again, and when he did so, his tone was less threatening. 'However, I am not merely offering you protection, Mr Harper. I can be of service to you in many other ways too, which may be useful to you in your, ah- unusual line of work, shall we say. My men can deliver you to other places along the coast - of this country and others if necessary - so that you are not continually transiting through Bangkok airport. I can also assist with any passports, visas, and travel documents that you might need.'

'As you say, that may well be very useful to me, but let me think about it first,' Harper said, playing for time.

'Of course, but you would be wise not to think about it too long.'

'I'll give you my answer within the week. How shall I contact you?'

'Oh, don't worry, Mr Harper, we'll contact you.'

CHAPTER 7

Three days later, back in Pattaya and still considering his options after the disconcerting encounter with Colonel Channarong, Harper was surprised to receive a hand-delivered invitation from the Saudi HOC asking him to return to the Embassy for a meeting about a project that the accompanying note described only as 'something mutually advantageous'.

Figuring that he had nothing to lose by hearing what the Saudis had to say, Harper drove to Bangkok that afternoon. He parked his truck close to the Saudi embassy and realised almost immediately that two men were following him. They were Thais, not Saudis, stockily built, and though they were in civilian clothes, they had the demeanour of military men. However, they were not particularly good at their job, since Harper had spotted them at once. He concluded they were Channarong's goons, detailed to keep an eye on him, and decided to give them the slip.

He strolled slowly around one of the main tourist areas, encouraging them to think he was unaware of the tail and merely taking in the sights on an afternoon stroll. Eventually he paused at the kerbside, ostentatiously checking his phone while pedestrians around him crossed the busy road and the followers hung back behind him, trying to look inconspicuous.

Just as the lights went to green and the traffic began to move, Harper suddenly sprinted across the road and ducked down an alley while the cacophony of car horns behind him showed that the followers were running foul of the traffic as they tried to chase him. He ran to the end of the alley, went right, right and right again and was in time to see the back view of one of his pursuers at the end of the first alley. Deciding to give them enough time to give up the search and leave the area, he ducked through an entranceway beneath a battery of air conditioning units fixed to the outside wall and found himself in what, according to the sign over the door, was the Bangkok Medical Museum.

Harper paid the five baht entrance fee to an ancient man with a wispy, Ho Chi Minh beard and walked through to the far end of the museum. He saw at once the reason for the multitude of air conditioning units, for the place was a cross between a morgue and a nineteenth century freak show or cabinet of curiosities. Suspended from the ceiling and lined up in tight-packed rows were Perspex boxes and specimen jars containing all manner of skeletons, mummified bodies and foetuses preserved in formalin. There were a number of desiccated corpses, their leathery faces contorted in their death agonies, with carefully hand-lettered signs next to each one proclaiming them to be the bodies of men executed by capital punishment after committing various hideous crimes. There were still-born Siamese twins, a foetus with a grossly swollen head, another that was covered in black hair as dense as a wolf's pelt, and one with skin that was an angry red colour and diamond-patterned like crocodile hide. If there had ever been any medical value in these exhibits, that was long in the past and they were now merely bait to lure in jaded Thais and curious tourists.

Harper gave himself another ten minutes then walked back towards the entrance. He stood in the shadow of the entranceway while he scanned the street in both directions, then stepped outside and headed back the way he had come, still alert for any indication that he was being watched or followed.

He made his unhurried way to the Saudi Embassy, where a different guard was on duty from the time he had last visited, but the mention of an appointment with the HOC was enough to see him ushered through the marble-floored lobby and into the receiving room where the HOC was already waiting for him.

'I'm glad you accepted my invitation, Lex,' he said. 'As I told you at our last meeting, knowledge is power. Since we last met, I have learned a great deal about you, some bad things, but mostly good. Interestingly I discovered that we are not the only ones who have been looking into you, for one of our sources told us that someone in the Thai military has also been taking a close interest in your activities and comings and goings.'

He waited for a reaction, but Harper kept his expression neutral and said nothing.

'Anyway, in gratitude for the service you have rendered to the Kingdom by rescuing the young princes, my leaders in Saudi Arabia have asked me to convey an invitation for you to visit our country as our honoured guest. As well as allowing us to offer you our finest hospitality, it will also provide an opportunity for you to meet some of our operational people in the same specialist line of work as yourself. If you are willing and,' he permitted himself a small smile, 'your current employer raises no objections, we have a proposition that I think you may find interesting. It would prove very lucrative for you, making use of your unusual skills and talents, and should also ultimately provide an opportunity to remove a source of nuisance to us both.' He paused. 'Although the young princes are safe, the man who had them held captive is continuing to blackmail their fathers. He claims, and I have no reason to doubt it, that he has film of the boys injecting themselves with the heroin his men enslaved them with, but, using his access to Thai intelligence sources and covert filming, he has also obtained compromising images of them drinking alcohol and having sex with prostitutes.' His expression showed his distaste. 'Obviously it's not at all the sort of thing that the Mutaween - our religious police - nor the Committee for the Promotion of Virtue and the Prevention of Vice would approve of, and it's also definitely not something the Kingdom would wish to see publicised.'

He again paused, waiting for Harper to comment, but Harper still preferred to keep his counsel, wanting to see all the cards the HOC held before showing his own hand.

'You may wonder why I'm telling you all this,' the HOC said, 'but our interests and yours might well coincide on this, because I have a feeling you've already made the acquaintance of the man I'm talking about. You know Colonel Channarong of the Thai Airborne Forces, do you not?' He smiled. 'I see from your expression that you do. So his elimination would solve a problem for both of us but we shall have to tread very carefully, Lex, because in the course of our enquiries about him, we also discovered that Colonel Channarong is a US "Person of Interest", or in other words, a man identified as being of potential future use to the United States. As you may know, there are many such Persons of Interest in a multitude of countries around the world, all run by handlers from the CIA and all paid a US dollar retainer to ensure their support for US policies, if ever or whenever it should be needed. We have a close alliance with the US, of course, but they are equally close allies of the Thais, so any visible attempt to target Channarong might well lead to American intervention or retaliation, which we - and you - would find uncomfortable, hence our interest in an "off-the-books" operative such as yourself.' He spread his hands. 'So there you have it, Lex. I've given you a lot to think about, I know, but whether or not you ultimately decide to take part in our endeavours, it will be the Kingdom's pleasure to be your host at our most luxurious Red Sea resort. We have an aircraft standing by to take you there.'

Harper inclined his head in acknowledgment. 'It's a very tempting offer and I'm grateful to you for it, but the small problem I have with Colonel Channarong means it may not be wise for me to be seen to be attempting to leave Thailand at the moment.' He chose his words carefully, not wanting to cause offence.

The HOC broke into a broad smile. 'Then we must make sure that you are not seen to be doing so, yes?' He glanced at his watch, a gold Patek Philippe that must have set him back around $100,000 US. 'I'll arrange travel under diplomatic cover for you. If you return here at - shall we say six this evening? - all the arrangements and the necessary paperwork will be in place. You will not have time to return to your base in Pattaya before then, of course, but please rest assured that a personal shopper will be at your disposal when you arrive in my country and any clothes or other items you may need - even a new watch,' he said, 'for I noticed you admiring mine, will be provided with the compliments of the kingdom.'

Harper smiled to himself, he was starting to like the way the Saudis conducted business. The combination of a few days scuba diving in the Red

Sea, a potentially lucrative op for the Saudis and, even better, the prospect of removing the threat to his Thai lifestyle that Channarong posed, was more than enough to overcome any reluctance he might have felt about decamping to Saudi Arabia. He duly presented himself at the embassy at six that evening, carrying only his usual bug-out bag, and was at once whisked away to the airport in a chauffeur-driven, top of the range Mercedes 500 with tinted windows and diplomatic plates.

When he reached the airport, the driver pulled up at a discreet gate in the perimeter fence, used by favoured diplomats and those with sufficient wealth or celebrity to by-pass the tedious formalities of airport departures. The security guard cast a cursory eye over the driver's papers and the darkened interior of the Merc, then saluted and signalled for the gate to be opened. Harper was driven to a compound on the far side of the airfield where a Royal Saudi Air Force Gulfstream jet was waiting. Harper jumped out, climbed the aircraft steps and settled himself in an opulent leather seat, the size of a substantial armchair.

The pilot was British and looked to be former military. He greeted Harper and then went back to the cockpit, leaving Harper in the care of the flight attendant, an Irish blonde holding a bottle of chilled Dom Perignon already poised over a crystal glass. 'Why not?' Harper said with a grin, 'it would be a pity to waste it.'

He was the only passenger as the jet was cleared for take-off and roared down the runway en-route to the Kingdom of Saudi Arabia. Colonel Channarong's deadline for Harper to respond to his proposal would expire while he was away, but pushing away the thought that it might be a long time before he felt safe to return to Thailand and his home in Pattaya, he settled back in his seat.

The plane began to descend after just two hours in the air, and Harper knew that it was a nine hour flight to Riyadh. Problems?' he said to the attendant.

'No, just another three passengers to collect from Singapore and then we're non-stop to Saudi.'

When the jet had landed at Changi and taxied across to the secure compound where private jets discreetly loaded and unloaded their passengers, Harper saw another Mercedes 500 with tinted windows waiting. Three women, clearly Saudi but in full hair and make up, dripping diamonds and dressed from head to toe in Western haute couture, emerged from the limo and walked up the steps, while their chauffeur carried their numerous bags. They greeted Harper with smiles, then settled themselves at the back of the jet where, the attendant poured them champagne which was quickly quaffed.

He dozed for much of the flight, only coming alert when the pilot's voice came up on the intercom, announcing that they would be entering Saudi airspace in fifteen minutes. The Saudi women at once put down their champagne glasses and one by one, disappeared into the loo. When each one re-emerged, the haute couture and make up were no longer visible, concealed beneath the shapeless black cloak, hood and mesh face-mask of a burqa.

When they had landed at King Khalid airport in Riyadh, protocol required that the women should wait deferentially until the male passenger had left the aircraft, before disembarking themselves. Harper walked down the aircraft steps where he was greeted by a Saudi driver in military uniform. While the Saudi women made their way into the terminal, Harper was ushered into a Landrover in desert camouflage but was driven only a few hundred yards across the airfield to a waiting Puma helicopter, its rotors already turning.

Harper jumped aboard and was flown to a Saudi airbase on the Red Sea coast, where a driver in the traditional flowing white Saudi *thawb* robes and *keffiyah* head-dress then whisked him away in an air-conditioned limousine to a man-made, luxury oasis on a private beach a few miles away. There were lodges and villas surrounding the main building of a complex that housed a seven-star hotel, with a series of restaurants, an Olympic-size swimming pool and the most lavishly equipped spa Harper had ever seen. The whole of the complex was covered by air-conditioned eco-domes that maintained the temperature at a mild low seventies Fahrenheit, compared to the furnace-like heat outside, where it could reach one hundred and twenty. The sound of flowing water was everywhere, with rills and fountains fed by an unseen desalination plant that irrigated the lush grass carpeting the whole area, and the gardens where date palms and other exotic fruit grew.

Guests could use jet-skis, snorkel or dive on the coral reef just off-shore, or enjoy a host of other facilities, and though Harper was aware of a few other people, the area was so large and the lay-out of the complex so carefully planned, that it was rare to encounter more than two or three others.

He took full advantage of the facilities to complete his recovery from the nightmare of heroin addiction and withdrawal, and rebuild his strength and fitness to its previous levels. After a few days of working out in the on-site gym, swimming, scuba diving, eating the finest food and spending long nights in untroubled sleep, he was feeling fitter than he had for several months. He was just wondering how long the Saudis would leave him to enjoy himself before they began looking for a quid pro quo, when a young servant knocked on his door and escorted him to the Maglis, the central meeting room for the complex. As he entered, he saw a young man, dressed in traditional Bedu clothing, who looked vaguely familiar, though he couldn't place him at first. The young man smiled at his expression. 'You do not recognise me Lex? I am not surprised, I looked rather different the last time we met.'

'Faisal!' Harper said. 'You're right, I didn't recognise you, though in my own defence, what with the layers of dirt and the effects of the heroin, you weren't looking your best, back then. I'm glad to see you've recovered so well.'

'I have come to thank you for saving my life from that hell-hole in Bangkok. Thanks to you, and the blessings of Allah, I am now clean of those filthy drugs and responding well to treatment. However my brother has not been so fortunate. He is still a slave to heroin and continues to resist what the specialists tell him and try to do for him. So only I am able to be here to thank you in person and I assure you that whatever the future brings for you and me, I and my family will always be with you, in person or in spirit. Now, do you have everything you need here?'

'Everything and more, thank you, I've been treated like a prince - and you know what that feels like, don't you?' Harper said with a grin.

'Very well my friend,' Faisal said. 'Go well and if you ever have need of my help in anything, it is yours.'

When Harper entered the gym for his daily work-out the following morning, he was surprised to see a beautiful young Saudi woman already going through her paces on the apparatus. Even more surprisingly, he noticed a pistol in a military-issue shoulder-holster on the bench behind her, partly concealed by a towel. He studied the woman with renewed interest. Her eyes were so dark they looked almost black in the subdued lighting of the gym, her jet-black hair was tied back in a most un-Saudi-like ponytail and she was wearing a tight-fitting track-suit that showed every contour of her body. As he set up the equipment for his own routine, he noticed that she was working through a tough programme but using light weights and low resistance to avoid building muscle while keeping the body supple and strong.

Lex began his own work-out, steadily building up the weights and the repetitions, but all the while he kept a surreptitious eye on his companion. As he did so, he became aware of a small, dark-skinned and very muscular man wearing a karate style track-suit who had slipped into the gym behind him and was now sitting quietly in a corner, almost motionless except for the occasional straightening of the black silken belt tied around his waist.

They continued working out, both very aware of the other, but studiously avoiding any overt contact.

Harper sat near the woman on a bench, as they sipped water and slowly cooled down. The woman kept glancing towards him and finally said 'May I introduce myself? I am Laiya bint Salman.'

'And I'm Lex,' Harper said, 'Lex Harper.' He nodded towards the man sitting in the corner. 'He doesn't say much, does he? Not that it's any of my business, but what's his story, exactly?

'He is called Saif - the name means Sword in my language - and he is my mentor, guardian, adviser and protector. He keeps me chaste-' she gave Harper an ambiguous smile as she said it, which combined with her low, husky voice, set his pulse racing a little faster, '-by discouraging the attentions of unsuitable men, and sometimes suitable men also. My potential suitors tend to fear him and with good reason, because he can be merciless. Occasionally, I listen to what he has to say but more often than not, I tend to ignore him.' Again there was the conspiratorial smile.

'He was appointed my guardian by my father when I was just a baby and he has been at my side always. He was even with me at Benenden in England - the only man at a school for the daughters of royalty, billionaires and oligarchs - and at my finishing school in Switzerland, where the girls all loved him. His duty to me will not end until I am married, when my husband will take over the responsibility, unless I am disgraced or killed before then, in which case Saif will have to avenge me and then kill himself.'

'Not a job with prospects, then,' Harper said.

She laughed. 'Possibly not. As you may know, in my country the girls marry very young. I am already a long way past the time when by our customs, I should have been married, so Saif should already have retired and be tending his gardens. He has no family but me and he would enjoy some peace and quiet, but sadly for Saif, though not for me, I am not ready to become a loyal submissive Saudi bride just yet. '

'Is Saif your only bodyguard?'

'Yes, but he's much more than just a bodyguard. Not only has he taught me the arts of diplomacy and the ways of various cultures, but from when I was very young he also instructed me in the traditions and skills of the Arab warrior. He has made me proficient in unarmed and armed conflict and I can use a large array of weapons - in fact everything from knitting needles to hand-held Surface to Air Missiles.'

'Impressive,' Harper said. 'My grandmother could be pretty lethal with a pair of knitting needles, but a SAM missile was definitely well above her pay grade!'

She smiled. 'I also persuaded Saif to let me attend the Saudi-Arabian Special Forces Selection Course.'

'And did you pass?'

She nodded. 'With honours. So, now I am a Major-General in the Royal Saudi Special Forces.' As she said it, she yawned and stretched, showing off every curve.

'Very pleased to meet you, Major-General,' Harper said, hiding his surprise. 'I never got beyond Warrant Officer myself.'

'In the SAS?'

He shook his head. 'The Parachute Regiment, but now I'm a civilian, a security consultant.'

'A description that covers a multitude of activities,' she said. 'But call me Laiya, please. And just because I have now told you all my secrets does not mean I would not like you to become one of my suitors, if you find me attractive.'

Harper glanced at Saif and saw his lips twitching as he tried to suppress a smile. 'After what you've already told me about Saif's way with a suitor, I think I'll take a rain check on that for now, thanks

Laiya, but you never know, I might just try my luck sometime.'

'As long as you are aware of the potential consequences, I think I would welcome that, though there is one further thing I should tell you. My guardian's favourite weapon is the silken strangling rope he wears round his waist. He keeps it for the unsuitable men who chase after me. He learned the arts of its use from some obscure religious sect in the Himalayas and he has used it before on at least a couple of occasions. I hope you don't find all this too off-putting.' She glanced across at Saif and then back at Harper, once more with a mischievous smile playing around her lips. 'See, even now he cannot keep from touching his rope.'

Harper returned her smile but found himself moving a little further away along the bench as he did so.

Before they parted, Laiya asked him to meet her in the Maglis later that day. When he did so, he found Saif there with her, still wearing his silk belt, sitting quietly to one side, but close enough to listen intently to everything that was said.

'I have a confession to make, Lex,' Laiya said, as soon as he sat down. 'I wanted to meet you and evaluate you, so our meeting this morning was not entirely coincidental.'

'I'd guessed as much.' Harper said. 'I've very much enjoyed my stay here but I learned a long time ago that there's no such thing as a free lunch.'

She inclined her head in acknowledgement. 'I believe our Head of Chancery at the embassy in Bangkok mentioned the possibility of a joint operation to remove a source of nuisance to all of us?'

'It was mentioned,' Harper said, 'but not in any detail.'

'Well, in fact we have in mind a series of three operations in which your skills could be very valuable to us. I am the nominated commander of those missions, but you will need to discuss this with the head of our special operations team. His cover name is Anwar.'

'And where will I find him?'

She smiled. 'In an office on the top floor of this building.'

Harper grinned back. 'Is there anyone in this resort at the moment who isn't involved in special operations?'

'Only the waiters, chefs and housemaids, and even they've all been security screened. Come.' Still tracked by Saif, she led Harper out of the Maglis and up a marble staircase to the upper floor. She knocked on a door at the end of the corridor and stepped back to allow Harper to enter first.

A man wearing the uniform of a Major in the Special Security Services division of the Royal Saudi Land Forces looked up from his desk, then stood up and gave the Arab greeting '*As salaam alaikum.*'

Harper made the traditional reply '*Wa alaikum a salaam.*'

'I'm Anwar,' he said, 'welcome.' He pressed a button on his desk and an aide hurried in with tiny cups of treacle-like, heavily ginger-flavoured black coffee and a dish of fresh dates. After drinking the customary polite two cups, Lex shook the cup to indicate his thirst was quenched.

As was the Saudi way, Anwar was in no hurry to address the purpose of their meeting and spent ten minutes making small talk with Harper about his stay at the resort and the delights of the Red Sea before getting to the point. In common with much of the Saudi elite, he had obviously been educated at an English public school, and spoke excellent, if still slightly accented, English.

'Lex,' he said at last, 'let us understand each other. The kingdom of Saudi Arabia is of course a rich and powerful nation, and, with the exception of the US, Russia and China, we spend more on defence than any country in the world. However - and I'm speaking frankly in the knowledge that this conversation is absolutely confidential.' He waited for Harper's nod before continuing. 'The lion's share of that expenditure has been on conventional weapons and forces, and our expertise in special forces operations and black ops has languished behind several other countries, including our traditional regional rivals, Iran and Israel. However, we can be very patient when it suits us and we are willing to learn from those with greater expertise, even when they are enemies. So we have studied the way other countries carry out their black ops. The Iranians often operate through proxies such as Hezbollah, providing weaponry, intelligence and other support, including advisers, but remaining in the background. The Israelis, by contrast, have little use for proxies. They are very methodical in pursuit of their objectives and utterly ruthless. They go in all guns blazing, do the job, take the flak and do not care what the world thinks of them, secure in the knowledge that their US allies will protect them from any backlash. American backbones, of course, are stiffened by an unholy alliance of the Zionist lobby and the born-again fundamentalist Christians itching for the US to provoke another Arab-Israeli war that will fulfil their prophecy that it will trigger "The Rapture".' He smiled and shook his head. 'And the West talks about Muslim extremists. We are nothing compared with the Zionists.'

Harper listened but said nothing. He cared little for politics, all he needed to know was what was required of him, and he was happy enough to sit and wait so he smiled and nodded amiably.

'The Russians are different,' continued Anwar. 'They try to carry out black ops secretly but their operatives are poorly trained and their methods clumsy, so the operations are often bungled or publicly revealed, like the attempted assassinations of Russian émigrés carried out on your own soil. The Americans themselves seem to suffer from some of the same failings and in any case, it is impossible to keep anything secret in Washington for long. We prefer the British way of operating, Lex. You carry out your black ops in the dark, as it were, leave quietly and when the balloon goes up, there is never a trace of a culprit and no evidence linking the op to you. We admire that sleight of hand and we aspire to act in the same way ourselves. I do know of some ops that have been carried out by, or on behalf of Britain, and I'm sure you could tell me of many others, were you to be so indiscreet, where often no one, not even the victims, realised exactly what had been done, let alone who had done it.'

Harper nodded again and smiled. And waited. He resisted the urge to look at his watch.

'So we have tried to absorb those lessons and now we have our own black operations team, modelled on the British approach, and as you've already discovered,' Anwar continued. He flashed a smile at Laiya, 'we even have female operators in our team. We have adapted the various selection methods used by other countries to toughen up the physical and mental attributes of the Saudi Bedu tribes. Our selection process is based on the strengths of the ancient Saudi warriors who spread the Word of Allah - blessed be his name - in the glorious past. We start by testing their ability to ride a camel and a horse, and then they have to live and travel for weeks in the vast desert wastes of our country. They also have to swim for long distances in the seas inhabited by all sorts of dangerous creatures, and finally they have to show their prowess with a rifle and other weapons. These are the ancient skills we look for. After that, we train them in the manner of modern operations. They have to be lethal in unarmed combat, able to handle all manner of weapons, be expert in one or more of a range of skills that include demolitions, sniping, surveillance and counter-surveillance, signals and battlefield trauma medicine. They must speak impeccable English, the language of the modern world. They must know how to conduct themselves in modern Western and Eastern society. And finally, they must be totally loyal to the House of Saud and to the country of Saudi Arabia. We have help from our friends to train them in all this because we know that time is important if we are to catch up with our rivals, and I would not be surprised if you were to come across a familiar face or two in the unlikely event you were ever to visit our training facility.'

Harper's smile was getting strained. It was clear that Anwar loved the sound of his own voice and while what he was saying was interesting enough, it was pretty much irrelevant.

Anwar was oblivious to Harper's discomfort as he continued his lecture. 'However, our personnel have not yet reached the levels of expertise and experience that you and your British colleagues possess - how could they when they have been training for only a few years and have very little combat experience? ' He gave a broad smile and spread his hands wide. 'So there you have it, Lex. We can offer you an opportunity to use your unique set of skills and talents, plus your knowledge of certain geographical areas, in matters of the utmost importance to us. We aim to launch joint operations using our own black ops team, in partnership with yourself and any additional personnel that you wish to bring in. Should you agree to take part - and should the agency which normally has first call on your services raise no objections to that - you will be extremely well rewarded. I am authorised to offer you a fee of one million American dollars - half in advance, the balance on completion - payable in gold, cash, or by transfer to any bank account anywhere in the world, as you prefer. Will you work with us?'

Harper wanted to cheer now that Anwar had finally got to the point, but he simply smiled. 'I thought you'd never ask. But I'd obviously appreciate a bit more information on the ops you're planning.'

Anwar and Laiya exchanged a glance. 'I cannot discuss the second operation at this point,' Anwar said, 'because it is at a very delicate stage, but the first one will target a group of Somali pirates.'

'Somali pirates? I thought that was all over now.'

'So did we. The increased NATO patrols and a series of air raids targeting the pirates' havens had seen the rate of incidents off the Somali coast and the Gulf of Aden drop to about a tenth of what it had been five years ago. However, there has recently been a marked resurgence, fuelled not just by the collapse of the Somali economy - that has never been much more than what I think you British call a "basket case" anyway - but also by the growing influence of Islamic terrorists, Al Shabaab in particular. They have infiltrated southern Somalia and are moving steadily north and they are not only extorting protection money from the local warlords but also forcing them back into piracy and demanding a share of the ransoms they collect from hijacked ships.'

'But it isn't just terrorists,' Laiya said. 'The pirates are also being funded by a stock exchange in the Somali city of Harardhere where, probably by no coincidence, Al Shabaab has a strong presence. It's not exactly the Square Mile of the City of London, but investors in Harardhere can buy and sell "piracy futures": shares in forthcoming attacks and hijackings. Somali expatriates, mostly in North America, have also been providing funds, equipment and information on ship movements, either in return for a share of the profits or simply to provide an income for relatives still living in Somalia.'

Harper was about to make a comment along the lines of 'brains and beauty' or 'not just a pretty face' but figured it wasn't the time or place for levity so he simply nodded.

'The pirate operations are increasingly sophisticated,' said Anwar. 'They even use currency-counting machines - exactly the same technology that banks and foreign exchange bureau use - supplied by corrupt currency dealers in Dubai. They aren't the only pirates in pin-striped suits. Insurance companies, in particular, have greatly increased their profits by raising insurance premiums for shipping because of the threat of piracy, yet they haven't required the companies to take even a single precaution to make hijacking more difficult, since the occasional ransoms they have to pay are dwarfed by the additional profits they are making. The shipping companies themselves routinely ignore the guidelines set by NATO and the IMCTC - the Islamic Military Counter Terrorism Coalition established by our Defence Minister Mohammad bin Salman Al Said - to minimise the risk of pirate attacks, since they involve additional expenditure. As always, the shipping companies prefer to cut their costs to the bone and take their chances with the pirates, secure in the knowledge that, although their crews may be captured, abused and even killed in the meantime, the insurance companies will eventually pay a ransom and the owners will get their ships back.'

Anwar was back in lecture mode and Harper ground his teeth again to stop himself yawning.

'International patrols of Somali waters like the NATO flotilla are there purely to deter private attacks and they ignore any other illegal activity taking place. The lack of any credible Somali patrols - they have no ships and no men to crew them even if they had - also allows foreign trawlers to empty their seas of fish, an annual harvest of tuna, lobsters and prawns estimated to be worth 300 million US dollars. Even worse, there is also a thriving trade in toxic waste. Foreign corporations, most of them front companies for the Italian and Russian mafia, are making fortunes by dumping millions of tons of toxic waste, even including nuclear waste, in Somali waters with complete impunity. Anyway, our own particular interest in this increased pirate activity is that twelve months ago, a supertanker owned by the Saudi Arabian Aramco oil company, loaded with highly flammable gasoline, was hijacked by pirates in the Gulf of Aden. We were forced to pay a $20 million ransom. I know,' he said, clocking Harper's expression. 'Paying ransoms is never a good idea since it merely encourages further hijackings but this was a decision made at a very high level, either encouraged by the insurance underwriters or perhaps seeking to minimise the loss of face involved in being held to ransom by people we have always regarded as barbarians. The ransom payment was made up of large denomination US dollar bills, wrapped in sealed plastic sacks. It was supposed to be dropped onto the deck of the pirate's mother-ship from a helicopter but, due to the fear or incompetence of the helicopter crew, it fell short of its target and landed in the sea.' He gave a cold smile. 'That crew has now been reassigned to much less pleasant duties than flying helicopters. The Somalis claimed that the ransom money sank before it could be retrieved and so we were forced to repeat the exercise and pay the money for a second time. However, our intelligence sources later established that the Somalis had in fact collected both ransom payments. This caused our government a considerable amount of embarrassment, as you can imagine.'

'Hence the desire for some pay-back,' Harper said. 'Though if the ransom hadn't been paid in the first place ...'

'Indeed,' Anwar said. 'I advised against it, but my advice was ignored.'

'So, including the one you're going to tell me about later, that's two tasks,' Harper said. 'And the third?'

'The one dearest to your own heart: eliminating the man who has been blackmailing two members of our royal family and, I gather, is also trying to blackmail you.'

'You wouldn't be leaving that op to last just to make sure that I participate in the other two, would you, Anwar?' Harper said with a sly smile.

'It is simply a matter of priorities, my friend, but at the due time, rest assured that whatever resources, equipment, funding or other support you need for that op will be provided without hesitation. In addition to the fee that we have already agreed, you will find us not ungenerous in respect of a completion bonus, when all the operations have been successfully concluded.'

'I'm grateful to you, Anwar,' Harper said. 'Generosity is always pleasing, but your help in eliminating a man who has proved to be a problem for both of us will be all the additional reward I need.'

Anwar stood up and shook Harper's hand. 'We look forward to working with you, Lex.'

CHAPTER 8

Later that afternoon, Harper was taken direct to the Saudi black ops team's base at Tabuk, close to the Red Sea and the borders of Jordan and Israel. Laiya had already set up a planning meeting for him with the members of her special operations team who had been chosen for the op. The men all seemed to have developed the ingrained self-confidence shared by Special Forces the world over, and were quite willing to fight their corner against their senior officers and NCOs when necessary. The only concession to their military background was to throw in an occasional '*Sidi*' - 'Sir' in Arabic - when they were making a point quite forcibly to someone of more senior rank.

Laiya then briefed them on the pirates SOPs: Standard Operating Procedures. 'Their preferred method is to use small, armed, fast attack craft to force target vessels of high value to stop,' she said. 'They are then boarded and taken close to the Somali coast, near the pirates' home villages, where the crew are taken ashore and kept in the sort of conditions that I'm sure you can imagine, until a ransom is paid. Each attack craft has a two-man crew, one overseeing the high-powered outboard engines while the other crew member is a weapons man, in charge of either rocket propelled grenades, medium machine guns or even just an AK 47. The target vessels are almost invariably unarmed and the threat from these weapons is usually enough to force the crews to surrender. The actions on target used by the pirates are to circle the chosen vessel and order it to stop. If it does not immediately comply, the weapons man will fire a couple of warning shots and if this still does not have the desired effect, he will put rounds onto the target. The whole operation is overseen from a mother-ship, usually a previously captured trawler or merchant ship, which waits further out in the Indian Ocean, watching everything on radar and directing the attack craft by radio, thus ensuring that the pirate leaders are well out of harm's way if the attack goes wrong or the attack craft are intercepted by warships.'

'One other thing,' Harper said. 'There is a NATO task force in the area but rather than enforcing the law of the sea, they appear to be operating a no-arrest, no-kill policy with regards to the Somali pirates. If the warship crews encounter them, they merely disarm them and even make sure they have enough water, food and fuel to make it back to the coast safely. So no one should be very surprised if the same crews then re-arm and return to the sea to carry out further hijackings.'

After intense discussions, they eventually came up with what seemed to Harper to be an eminently workable plan. It was vital that it had come from the shop floor; the final plan had to be theirs, not one that had been foisted on them, because if it was their own, they would buy into it much more readily and strive even harder to make it succeed.

Winding up the reviewing session, he reminded the team that they had agreed on a three phase operation. 'Phase 1: we lure the pirates' attack craft close enough to destroy them.

'Phase 2: we force the pirate leader to abandon the mother ship and head back to his base onshore. We then destroy the mother-ship, preventing its use in any future pirate attacks.

'Phase 3: our attack team, myself and twelve of you, land after dark, attack the leader's house - the pirates' "Mr Big" - kill him and then withdraw.'

'One last thing,' Laiya said. 'The name of this Mr Big, as you call him, Lex, is known to us. He is Abu Moussa, and not only do we know who he is, we also know where he lives, and have satellite imagery of it.'

Harper grinned. 'Then what are we waiting for? However, whatever happens, we can't simply take the easy option and destroy him and his mother-ship at sea. If you are going to send a message that you are a serious force to be reckoned with, so that not just Abu Moussa's gang, but all the Somali pirates understand the price to be paid for any further hijackings of Saudi ships, you have got to be seen to be delivering that message. If we kill him at sea, there are unlikely to be any surviving witnesses, so we have to force him home and then kill him on land at his headquarters. If we do that, there will be no shortage of people who have witnessed the attack and before long, everyone in Somalia as well as a lot of other people around the region will know who killed him.' He gave a grim smile. 'So we know where he lives and we have imagery of the target, let's go get him.'

The vessel that the Saudis were using for the attack was the absolute top of the range in every way. Called *Al Shaheen* - 'The Hawk' in English - the ship appeared to be one of the elegant, hyper-expensive yachts that billionaires, oligarchs and the rulers of oil-rich states used to flaunt their wealth, but its luxurious exterior concealed a hidden purpose: it was the Saudis' special operations launch vessel, designed to operate anywhere in the world.

Laiya took Harper down to the dock where the yacht was berthed. It was an impressive sight, towering above them as they stood on the dock, with the sunlight reflecting from its gleaming, pristine white hull, dazzling Harper as he craned his neck to look up at the superstructure. 'It looks like a billionaire's super-yacht,' he said.

Laiya smiled. 'That was our intention and yet, despite its looks, it has all the strike capabilities of a warship.'

She showed him round, reeling off details of the specification, like a saleswoman trying to clinch a deal. 'It was designed in Sweden to our own very particular specification,' she said, 'and then built under conditions of the utmost secrecy in South Korea.'

They passed through the saloons and staterooms on the upper decks, all highly polished marble and exotic hardwoods, gold fittings and a ceiling studded with thousands of tiny diamonds to represent the stars in the night sky. Harper whistled. 'There's more bling here than a rappers' convention.'

'I'm not sure the ship's designers would be too pleased with that comparison,' Laiya said with mock severity. 'Below decks you'll find it's much more functional than decorative.' She led him to a companionway that led to the heart of the ship.

'The *Al Shaheen* has seven decks and a bridge,' she said. 'As you've seen, the top two decks consist of state rooms and reception areas for entertaining visiting VIPs. The third deck houses the operations and communication centre and the lower decks contain accommodation, mess areas, stores and armouries, including an armoured ammunition bay. One whole deck is given over to medical treatment, including two operating theatres and staff, with facilities equal to the best in any UK hospital, and we carry enough blood and plasma stores to treat the casualties of a major battle. All of this, of course, is well hidden behind the façade of a rich man's plaything. Any visitors on board see only what we wish to show them; everything else is off-limits. The ship also carries two distinct crews - the sailors and staff who operate the ship and entertain our rich guests, and our special ops team to strike at our enemies. Many people around the world welcome a Saudi super-yacht, seeing only the opportunity to make money, and they never look for the wolf in sheep's clothing.' She grinned. 'We like the subterfuge, just like you British. I think this is why your country's forces would like a new Royal Yacht to be commissioned, so they can have a strike capability like ours.'

'And what does that strike capability consist of?' Harper said.

'Everything you could wish for, short of a nuclear bomb,' Laiya said. 'The vessel is armed with a range of weapons that include cruise missiles, surface-to-air missiles, Gatling guns and ship-to-ship missiles for defence. On the keel there is a docking port for mini submarines and divers, and there are doors at the rear for launching rigid inflatable boats and the on-board landing craft. There is also a heli-deck, giving an over the horizon capability using the helicopter carried on board, which also doubles as a troop carrier. The hull of the ship is constructed of composite material and carbon fibre, shaped to give it a "stealth" profile that conceals it from enemy radar, and the parts of the hull external to vital components are protected by Kevlar panels. All the weapons are in hidden pods inside the hull and to maintain the ship's stealth profile, they are only deployed when ready to fire.'

'Pretty impressive,' Harper said. 'Are the engines similarly state of the art?'

'Definitely. The *Al Shaheen* is propelled by water jets powered by three diesel-electric pumps that give it almost silent running, even at the top speed of over seventy knots. The absence of propellers and the ship's shallow draft also allows us to work very close inshore when required.'

'Perfect,' Harper said. 'Let's get started and see if the ship lives up to the billing.'

The *Al Shaheen* eased away from its moorings that afternoon and, travelling in radar stealth mode to avoid alerting the NATO flotilla, cruised south down the Red Sea, heading for the Gulf of Aden. They kept to about thirty knots, less than half the ship's top speed, with four surveillance drones deployed invisibly high in the sky relaying images of the Eritrean and Yemeni coasts and the shipping using the waterway directly back to the operations centre. As Laiya had claimed, the yacht's three diesel-electric pumps worked almost silently, driving the yacht forward by injecting thousands of litres of water per second through nozzles at the rear of the ship.

The daytime heat was ferocious, well into the forties Celsius and, standing at the rail, watching bottlenosed dolphins surfing the pressure wave at the ship's bow, Harper was glad of the breeze the ship created as it cut through the waves. Off to his right he would see the barren sand dunes and parched scrub of the Eritrean coastal desert, with the mountains flanking the central plateau intermittently visible through the heat haze and dust.

He also caught occasional glimpses of tribes of Bedu trekking through the dunes beyond the coast. 'I'm always amazed how they survive in this kind of terrain, and in this kind of heat,' Harper said, as Laiya stood next to him at the rail of the ship.

'Most Europeans wouldn't last twenty-four hours,' Laiya said. 'But Arabs and Africans have been surviving and even thriving here for thousands of years. There is a lot of skill and a lot of knowledge and lore passed down from generation to generation, but it's also a matter of temperament. Europeans and Americans always seem to be in a rush, whereas we Arabs have learned the value of patience.' She glanced to the south where a fog-like bank was now spilling over the water from the desert shore. 'Especially in a sandstorm. I suggest we get below decks before it hits us.'

They hurried along the deck, but the sandstorm was upon them before they reached the sanctuary of the ship's air-conditioned interior. The storm turned bright daylight into dusk and though Harper wound his Arab *keffiyeh* scarf around his face, the stinging, gritty grains of sand found their way through every chink. He could feel sand on his lips and eyelids, and in his ears, and had to grope his way to the doorway by touch, since he could not see his hand in front of his face.

The storm cleared as quickly as it had arrived and the vistas of desert sand and rock reappeared. As they passed the Eritrean border with Djibouti, the terrain grew even harsher and more forbidding, with desert, rock and range upon range of mountains, virtually bare of vegetation.

The Yemeni coast, visible from the opposite side of the ship, was little more fertile. The *Tihama* - the narrow, semi-desert coastal plain - rapidly gave way to the forbidding highlands and mountains that made up ninety per cent of the country. Fringing the Empty Quarter of Saudi Arabia, Yemen had not a single permanent river and in the fearsome heat of summer, everything - rock, earth, buildings, livestock and people - seemed to be the colour of dust.

As Harper watched, he heard the roar of fast-jets and four Saudi warplanes screamed overhead and crossed the Yemeni coast. A couple of minutes later there were the vivid red-orange flashes of multiple bomb-blasts and missile strikes on an inland town. Gouts of oily black smoke began billowing upwards into the sky, just as the delayed sound of the distant explosions reached his ears.

He caught Laiya's eye. 'Perhaps best if we don't talk about what your country is doing to the Houthis and the Yemenis,' he said, 'Not exactly a fair fight, is it? Fast jets and Hellfire missiles against people armed with AKs if they're lucky and antique hunting rifles if they're not.'

Laiya gave him a baleful look. 'Of course you British know all about fighting fair in Yemen, don't you? I don't remember being told of much interest in human rights in the days when Aden was a British colony, a coaling station on the Empire route to India. Nor when British soldiers - your predecessors, Lex - were engaged in a brutal campaign against Yemenis fighting for their country's independence from Britain.'

'Very true, Laiya,' he said, 'but to be fair, that all ended half a century ago, whereas what Saudi Arabia is doing to Yemen is happening right here, and right now.'

She shrugged. 'What can I say, Lex? We're soldiers, aren't we? And what soldiers do is obey the orders they're given by their superiors, whatever they might privately think of them.'

Harper grinned. 'Which is dangerously close to what the Nazis were all saying at the end of the Second World War: "We were only following orders". Sorry,' he said, as he saw her face redden with anger. 'Ignore that last smart-arse remark, I was just pulling your chain.'

That evening they passed through the narrows of the Bab-al-Mandeb strait linking the Red Sea to the Gulf of Aden and the Indian Ocean. It was one of the busiest shipping lanes in the world and they passed an endless stream of container ships heading north towards the Suez Canal, laden with Chinese goods for Europe, while supertankers carrying Middle Eastern oil were travelling in the opposite direction.

They maintained speed through the night and by midday the next day they were off the coast of Somalia. In any other part of the world, the beautiful white sand, palm-fringed beaches would have made it a dream tourist destination but the only tourists who had set foot in Somalia in decades were adrenaline junkies and "adventure tourists" too young, dumb and full of come to realise the jeopardy they were placing themselves in. Riddled with drought, crime, corruption and food insecurity, Somalia was a failed state, run by warlords and criminal gangs, with Islamist terror groups like Al Shabaab a growing presence. There had been no direct US or UK involvement in the country since the "Blackhawk Down" disaster twenty-five years before. The economy was virtually moribund, the only growth industry being piracy, carried out by warlords, approved by the clan elders and largely supported by the local population since it gave some of them a cash income that no other activity could provide.

On board the *Al Shaheen,* the crew had already carried out a series of practice drills with the various weapons systems and had become more slick and proficient by the hour, while Lex and the troops delegated for the upcoming op continued to review and fine-tune the plan that they had devised.

They avoided the NATO naval flotilla with ease, since it was busy escorting supertankers in and out of the Gulf, and had no time to spare for luxury yachts, even when they were making directly for some very dangerous waters. Harper could imagine the conversation on the bridge of the warships in the flotilla, if they spotted the *Al Shaheen*: "If some half-witted billionaire wants to risk his yacht and his life in search of something exotic enough to tickle his jaded palate, who are we to stop him?"

The Saudi ship had now reached the favoured operating area of the Somali pirates. There was no breath of wind and the heat seemed even more intense on the eve of probable combat, with the blazing sun turning the ocean the colour of molten brass.

Switching off the stealth radar systems, they slowed the ship right down and waited for the pirates to take the bait. Their reaction was not long in coming. Within an hour, the *Al Shaheen*'s high definition radar was highlighting the blips of vessels approaching the yacht at high speed. At the same time, they were picking up radar emissions from further out to sea, which the radar operator quickly confirmed were coming from the pirates' mother-ship.

Soon they were being circled by four attack craft, their high-powered outboard motors churning the sea into white foam as they sped around the Saudi ship like Native Americans attacking a circled wagon train. Harper could see that men on two of the craft were armed with medium machine guns. He assumed that the other two would be carrying an RPG or something similar. At once, there was a call over the ship's radio ordering the Al Shaheen to stop. When this was ignored, one of the pirate vessels fired a long burst over the top of the ship. Laiya then ordered the skipper to bring the ship to a standstill while the pirates' attack craft continued to circle around it at top speed.

The yacht's wake faded away and as it rolled gently in the swell, still in the water, Harper ordered the stern doors to be opened to allow the pirates access. While three of the pirates' craft continued to circle the yacht with their weapons trained on it, Harper swiftly descended from the bridge and ran to the stern in time to see the fourth pirate vessel making a cautious approach.

As the pirates got closer to the stern dock, Harper, standing on a pontoon, was able to make out the faces of the two Somalis, who were very nervously trying to peer inside the ship. Harper gave a broad smile, gesturing for them to come in. They hesitated and then gingerly resumed their approach. They were concentrating on keeping their vessel safe, and by the time they had registered that Harper had calmly drawn an automatic pistol from the waistband of his jeans, he had shot both of them in the head.

As Harper had arranged with the weapons officers on the *Al Shaheen*, the sound of his shots triggered an immediate follow-up. The weapon pods on the sides of the hull rotated to reveal four electrically-powered Gatling guns. Remotely controlled from the weapons centre, the Gatlings spat fire at the rate of 6,000 rounds a minute, and completely destroyed the remaining three pirate boats in seconds, leaving the surface of the ocean empty but for debris, oil slicks and bloodstains that slowly dispersed and dissipated in the current. None of the pirates had got off even a single round in reply.

As the sound of the explosions died away, it was replaced by the whine of jet turbines as the helicopter scrambled steeply upwards from the heli-deck. As it climbed higher, the Weapons Officer switched on the long-range, high definition image intensifier. As soon as the target mother-ship was in sight, the images were relayed back to the operations room on the Shaheen.

When the trawler was in range the WO fired off an air-to-surface guided missile which he skilfully caused to land in the sea a handful of metres in front of his target. The waterspout from the missile soaked the trawler from stem to stern, and watching on the screen on the *Al Shaheen,* Harper and the others could see the resulting panic breaking out. They watched the terrified crew attempting to abandon ship, fighting each other to clamber aboard the remaining attack craft that were moored alongside.

To speed their departure, the WO fired off a second missile and this one struck the trawler with a blinding flash just behind the bow. As metal fragments spattered down around the mother-ship, things on the vessel turned really nasty, with one man using his weapon to shoot everyone in his path as he ran towards one of the attack-craft. He then killed a couple of the crew who were already on board with the engines running, gunned the boat and sped off, bouncing over the waves and leaving the remaining crew to their fate.

'That's the man we want,' Laiya said, 'that's the bastard Moussa. Don't lose him on the imager.'

While Moussa headed for the shore at top speed, his surviving men scrambled for the one remaining attack craft. Under orders from Laiya, the *Al Shaheen*'s Weapons Officer held off further fire until the attack craft had cast off from the mother-ship. It was so overloaded that waves were almost lapping over the gunwales of the craft and it made ponderous progress towards the shore. Laiya waited until it was a couple of hundred metres clear of the mother-ship before giving the order to resume fire. Two further missile strikes then hit the abandoned mother-ship. The first, just aft of the bridge, blew out part of the hull. The second, penetrating the engine room, caused a huge explosion that broke the ship's back. It slowly settled in the water, listing further and further to one side, then turned turtle and sank. Geysers of water and steam erupted around the stricken ship and when they cleared, it had disappeared from sight, leaving only pieces of debris and a widening oil slick to mark where it had been only moments before.

Harper barely noticed the disappearance of the mother-ship, all his attention focussed on the screen tracking Moussa's craft to the shore. He roared through the shallows and ploughed a furrow into the white sand as he beached his craft and abandoned it, his feet floundering in the soft sand as he ran up the beach and through the village. By now it was late afternoon and the pictures from the helicopter were being compromised by the setting sun, but Harper was able to make out just enough detail to see Moussa enter the single-storey complex of buildings which they had already identified as his headquarters.

'Right,' Harper said. 'We've got him hauled up and gone to ground, so we go ashore at midnight, lie up around the target and go in at first light to finish the job. Remember everyone in the village will be armed and they will fight to defend the man, if only because he bankrolls the whole area. So we go in quick, do the job, create a diversion and then get out, but most important of all, nobody gets left behind.'

Just before midnight, dressed in wet-suits, Harper, Laiya and the rest of the attack team transferred to the *Al Shaheen*'s landing craft. It cast off from the yacht and moved silently through the water towards the shore. In the darkness, its low hull would have been almost invisible to any but the most alert watcher on the coast. The attackers slipped over the side a couple of hundred metres from the shore, where the breaking surf was just visible as a faintly phosphorescent line. They swam the rest of the way in their wet-suits, towing their kit in waterproof bags behind them, and arrived with barely a noise or a ripple on the shore.

After checking out the area around the landing point, they readied themselves for battle. Harper could smell wood smoke from a couple of smouldering fires drifting on the breeze but the village was still and silent, and in complete darkness. Wearing Passive Night Goggles and moving in diamond formation, they navigated their way up the beach and then slipped silently between the houses, using the shadows and every scrap of cover. Quiet as they were, their movements set stray dogs to howling in the darkness. The noise echoed around the attack team, jangling Harper's nerves.

They took up their planned positions around the target: a cluster of outbuildings occupied by the rest of Moussa's gang-members. It formed a defensive perimeter around the house at the core of the complex that was Moussa's headquarters. Although more substantial than the palm-thatched mud-brick dwellings in the rest of the village, the outbuildings' walls of brick and breeze-blocks were unlikely to be much of a barrier to the powerful explosive charges the attackers carried. Through his night vision goggles, Harper could see that a couple of sentries had been posted on the roof of the complex but both of them were sound asleep.

Even for the most experienced combat troops, the period of waiting before an attack was launched was always the most difficult time, but Harper was impressed by the patience shown by the Saudis. They remained on hyper-alert but silent and motionless as the dark hours of the night slowly passed.

As the sun at last began to rise, putting a little warmth back into their chilled bones, Harper stole out of cover, approached the outbuilding that barred the way to Moussa's house and fixed a frame charge onto the wall of one of the buildings.

He muttered 'Standby, Standby,' into his throat microphone and then initiated the five second fuse. The charge went off with a muffled bang, imploding the wall into the building. The over-pressure caused by the blast killed everyone inside, bursting their lungs within their chests, and sent one of the sleeping sentries on the roof plunging to his death.

Without waiting to check the carnage, Harper led the way through the gap the blast had caused in the walls, followed by Laiya and two of the other Saudis, while the rest of the attack team remained outside, guarding the perimeter, killing the remaining sentry on the roof and exchanging fire with several villagers who had been woken by the blast and were now firing off bursts from their AK-47s. However their firing was wild and uncoordinated and little threat to the disciplined, aimed bursts of the Saudi attackers. They picked off a group of villagers who were attempting to launch a frontal assault on the attackers and any others who showed themselves for more than a split second found themselves coming under a deadly, withering fire.

Inside the compound, Harper kicked down the door of Moussa's HQ building, tossed a flash-bang through the doorway and followed it a heartbeat later, diving, rolling and coming up firing. Two of Moussa's bodyguards died instantly as Harper led Laiya and the other Saudi soldiers on into Moussa's inner sanctum. Less than ten seconds had elapsed since the frame charge was detonated and they found the pirate gang-leader still struggling to get out of his bed, while trying to bring his AK-47 to bear on the attackers. The naked woman who had been in bed with him was screaming the place down while trying to squeeze herself down between the bed and the wall.

Without even a momentary pause, Harper put a double tap into Moussa's head, while Laiya silenced the screaming woman with a stinging slap across the face and then immobilised her with plastic handcuffs. After checking that the rest of the building was clear, they searched the room and found several steel ammunition boxes hidden under the bed. Each of them was stuffed with Western currency - Euros, pounds, Swiss francs and US dollars - in high denomination notes.

Gesturing to the others to help, they dragged one of the boxes out into the open and began throwing the money it contained up into the air and over the remains of the outer wall where, caught and dispersed by the early morning breeze, the notes drifted all over the village, falling like manna from heaven among the incredulous villagers. Ignoring the continuing fire from the Saudi soldiers maintaining the perimeter, some of the villagers began emerging from cover and scrabbling in the dust, gathering up handfuls of notes - probably more money than they had seen in their entire lives.

'That will keep them busy, while we get out of here,' Harper said. He paused for a moment, looking at the remaining boxes of cash. 'There must be enough here to make even a Saudi oil sheikh pause for thought. Shame we can't take it with us, but we can't carry it and I'm not sure your Boss would be too happy if we did, because it might suggest our minds weren't entirely focussed on the task. Still, no sense in leaving it here for the pirates. They'll only be buying replacement craft and weapons with it.'

With Laiya's help, he emptied out the contents of all the other boxes, piling up a mound of banknotes. He took out his disposable lighter, set fire to the pile and waited for a few seconds to make sure it was fully alight. 'Right, job done, no need to hang about any longer,' he said.

Regrouping, they stormed back down through the heart of the village, using fire and movement, one group putting down covering fire while the others sprinted a few yards then dropped into cover to return the compliment. They kept up a barrage of vicious suppressing fire that took out any of Moussa's remaining men still putting up a fight and kept the heads of the rest well down. When they reached the shore, they eliminated any possibility of further pursuit by pouring fire into the two pirate attack-craft beached by Moussa and his surviving crew the day before. Rounds from the Saudis' semi-automatic rifles punched holes through the hulls, sending a blizzard of splinters into the air. Had anyone attempted to launch the craft after that, they would have sunk within seconds.

Harper, Laiya and her men waded out through the shallows and were picked up by the *Al Shaheen*'s landing craft, waiting just offshore, and carried back to the ship. Their only casualty was one of the attack team who had been slightly wounded by a ricochet from one of the villagers' AK-47s.

On board everyone was understandably jubilant, whooping and high-fiving each other. Harper and Laiya let them enjoy the moment for a while before calling them to order and reminding them that there was still much work to be done. 'You've done great today and earned your celebration,' Harper said, 'but you need to refocus quickly because there are bigger and probably harder tasks ahead.'

Laiya nodded. 'This was only the first phase of a three-stage operation. We head north at once, ready to begin planning the next phase.'

The *Al Shaheen* was already slicing through the water, its propulsive jets driving it at high speed away from Somalia and back towards the Red Sea and the Suez Canal, while its stealth profile continued to hide it from the radar of the patrolling NATO flotilla.

CHAPTER 9

While the *Al Shaheen* continued north, the ship's helicopter transferred Laiya and Harper direct to the Saudi black ops base in answer to an urgent summons from Anwar. When they walked into the briefing room where he was waiting, he wasted few words on congratulations for the success of phase one. 'The second op is now very much "Go" and we will value your involvement, Lex, not only because of your special skill-set, but also because we believe you know the area where the op will take place. To give you the background: the government of Saudi Arabia was recently approached by an intermediary bearing an offer from a Serbian mafia gang. In return for a payment of several million US dollars they are offering to supply us with a Tactical Nuclear device they have obtained.'

'Bloody hell,' Harper said. The Serb mafia was a very heavy-duty organisation. They were into everything; drug-peddling, arms-trafficking, armed robbery, smuggling, people-trafficking, protection rackets, prostitution and smuggling. In the early

2000s it was reliably estimated that they had a bigger budget, a larger army and better equipment than the Serbian state itself and they killed politicians, government ministers and even the Serbian prime minister with impunity. Although the Serbian police had made some high-profile busts in recent years, Harper knew that the Serb mafia was still the most powerful and dangerous organised crime group in Europe, even pushing the Sicilian mafia and the Ndrangheta – another Sicilian crime group - out of the drug trade in Italy.

'Nuclear weapons is a bit of a step up even for them,' he said. 'How convinced are you that they really do have a Tac Nuke?'

'We know the device is real, because we asked for and were given the serial number and we traced that back to a Spetsnaz installation in the former DDR - East Germany - in 1989, just before the fall of the Berlin Wall. The device is definitely viable, because according to open source NATO documents, these things have a shelf life of over fifty years. What has particularly focussed our minds is intelligence that suggests that in an attempt to start a bidding war between us, the Serbian gangsters have also offered the device to the Government of Iran. As you know, the Iranians are our greatest enemies and they would like nothing better than to turn the cities of the Kingdom to dust. The Iranians have already been talking to the sellers and our go-between insists that the endgame of those negotiations is near. So our greatest fear is that the device will end up in the hands of our hated enemies, the Iranians, and we believe that if they do get their hands on it, they will try to detonate it on Saudi territory in a location that will enable them to blame the Americans for the explosion. The presence of American troops and warplanes in the Kingdom - the Custodian of the Most Holy Places of Islam - has always been controversial among believers, and the Iranians believe that a nuclear explosion linked to the Americans would create such a backlash against the US that they would be forced to withdraw from the Arabian Peninsula. That would cause us real problems and would be a huge gain for our enemies.'

'And what will you do with the device if you are successful in getting hold of it? Harper asked.

'Oh, we would undoubtedly destroy it,' Anwar said, stone-faced.

'Really?' said Lex, trying but failing to keep the cynicism from his voice. 'Are you sure you wouldn't, for example, take a leaf out of the Iranian playbook and detonate the device near one of the Iranian Atomic Research Installations, creating the impression that, despite their protestations that their research is entirely devoted to civil nuclear power, they have been developing nukes? That would inevitably lead to the Israeli Air Force launching strikes to bomb the Iranians back into the dark ages.'

Anwar shrugged. 'All that is wild speculation, Lex, and as military men, our job is to deal in facts on the ground and leave policy and strategy to our political masters.' He held his gaze for a moment and then resumed, his tone brisk and no-nonsense. 'Now what do you know about Tactical Nuclear Devices?'

'Tac Nukes? Quite a lot. I trained with them when I was in the Parachute Regiment of the British Army. The ones I worked with were a two-stage device, the first stage was in effect a primer, the equivalent of one thousand pounds of TNT. That was used to detonate the second stage, the nuclear bit, which was equivalent to a bomb of twenty-five megatons. The two parts were man-portable. Stage one weighed about fifteen kilos and was the size of a shoebox; stage two weighed about fifty kilos and was the size of a medium suitcase. Once on target, they could be plugged together and after a series of warm-up tests, they could be detonated remotely, with the troops who delivered them hopefully having extracted to a safe distance from the site of the blast.' He gave a cynical smile. 'Or that was how they sold it to us anyway, but common sense told us that even Usain Bolt wouldn't be able to make a fast enough get away to avoid being cooked like an overdone steak. The Tac Nukes were to be used to target choke points and enemy troop and logistic areas, and they were considered to be "dirty bombs", throwing out a lot of radiation and rendering the area inhospitable for years afterwards. We were allowed to look but not touch but everyone involved knew that to take one of those on to the battlefield would effectively have been a suicide mission. For a couple of years, the boffins and Army brass were trying to decide the best way of delivering them to where they were needed, after all our air force and cruise missiles had been blown out of the sky. There was a difference of opinion as to whether to use a company of Paras - about a hundred men - to fight their way to the target area with the device in the centre, or whether to use a four-man SAS patrol to infiltrate the device covertly to the target. Even though we were never shown or told the results of the TACEVAL - the Tactical Evaluation Exercise - the SAS eventually won the argument hands down. With the inevitable exception of the senior officers in the Paras who had an unfailing appetite for volunteering their men for every mission going, and the more suicidal the better, since those were the ones where the most gongs were subsequently handed out to the officers, everyone else agreed that the SAS option was the more viable, partly because if it went wrong, instead of losing a company, you would only lose a four-man patrol.'

He gave a bleak smile. 'Anyway, that's what you'll be dealing with if the Saudi bid is successful. So I hope you'll be handling it with due care and attention.'

The *Al Shaheen* docked back at its Red Sea base that evening and within minutes Armourers were bringing aboard replacements for the missiles and munitions used against the Somali pirates, food and water stocks were being replenished, fitters were making repairs to the damaged sections of the hull, with a team of painters following behind them to restore the ship to its pristine condition.

With the full team now back at base, Laiya called a planning conference for first thing the next morning, involving Harper, the Captain and Weapons Officer of the *Al Shaheen,* and all the members of the Saudi black ops team allocated to the next operation.

When the planning session began, Laiya immediately started briefing them on the actions on arrival in Serbia, but after letting her speak for a couple of minutes, Harper felt he had to interrupt. 'With all due respect, Laiya, aren't we putting the cart before the horse here? I've got some major concerns about our transit through the Suez Canal and I feel that those should be addressed before we move on to the op itself. Can we not take the briefing in sequence, deal with the transit to Serbia in stages and then get to the actions on target once we've made sure that we're actually going to get there?'

Laiya pursed her lips in a gesture of annoyance but having thought about it for a few moments, she acknowledged the wisdom of what he was saying. 'Okay. We'll be heading north through the Red Sea and transiting the Suez Canal into the Mediterranean. The Canal consists of a series of lakes linked by man-made cuttings and although, as you all know, it has been dredged and widened to allow two-way traffic over part of its length in recent years, a long stretch of it is still one-way, with ships travelling in convoys and waiting in the lakes while vessels coming the other way pass through - all except the US military, of course, who use their alliance with Egypt as an excuse to jump the queue. It's typical American bullying - what is it they say "My way or the highway"?'

'Any way that we can also jump the queue?' Harper said.

'Of course, but we'll do it without threat and bluster, though with equally good results.'

'Bribery, in other words.'

She shrugged. 'We are Saudis and Saudi money talks, especially when people are desperately poor. The area is very heavily patrolled by the military because the Suez Canal is Egypt's main source of revenue, but the soldiers are poorly trained, poorly paid conscripts who have no real motivation to risk losing their lives for the sake of the elite in Cairo. A few dinars go a long way in such a situation.'

'And are there any speed restrictions?'

'None that need apply to us. We will travel at whatever speed we choose and when necessary our money will remove any bureaucratic or other obstacles that might hinder our passage. That is our usual way.'

Harper smiled. 'So that takes care of one problem but there is another: the Sinai Peninsula and North Sinai in particular, is a hotbed of fundamentalism. Many of the armed groups there are in the Iranian camp, and so have no reason to look kindly on any Saudi ship within range of their weapons. If they have wind that we will be passing through the Suez Canal they will have a field day unless we are prepared for it. So tell me that you've been monitoring comms traffic in the Peninsula for any suspicious chatter between the fundamentalists.'

He was met only by silence and blank looks, and shook his head in disbelief. 'Then you need to get on to it straight away. Get an AWACS plane up over the Red Sea and keep it airborne until this is sorted out. We may yet have to fight our way through, but even so, it's better than the alternative of a twelve-day trip around Africa to Gibraltar, by which time the Iranians would probably be on their way home with the Tac Nuke in their cabin baggage. We may have an entirely trouble-free transit of the Canal, but we can't rely on that and I think we need a "just in case" plan to cover the risk of fundamentalist attack. So I suggest we take four desert buggies on board the *Al Shaheen* and use them as a screen on land, two on each side of the vessel, while it is moving through the Canal. We can arm the buggies with anti-tank missiles such as Milans or the Soviet AT range of missiles, whichever you have on inventory, and we'll have our personal weapons of course. The weapons of choice for these bastards are vehicle-mounted SU 23 cannon, RCL recoilless rifles and 12.7 machine guns that are all usually carried on Toyota pick-ups. It is useless to think we can fly the heli against them, because the SUs will blast it out of the sky, so it'll be best to keep it in the hangar until we need it later. Instead we should deploy a couple of unmanned drones to give us over the horizon viewing as we travel along.

The SUs aren't a significant threat to the ship but the RCL recoilless rifle is another order of difficulty altogether. It fires a shell that was designed for use against armoured vehicles, but the ship is just a large armoured vehicle and the bad news is that the RCL's projectile will blow a hole in pretty much anything and then inject gases and molten metal into the target, killing and destroying everything inside. The good news is that the round flies low and slow and is not easy to aim off on a moving target - even one as big as a ship - providing it is moving fast enough, so that's a very good reason to bribe whoever we need to make sure the ship is moving fast through the Canal and is not left as a sitting duck in a queue of waiting vessels in the Great Bitter Lake or anywhere else. Now although we'll have our buggies as out-runners, they will be heavily out-ranged and out-gunned by the fundamentalists, so if trouble is brewing we will have to get close enough to see the whites of their eyes if we are going to prevail. Questions? Okay, thanks Laiya, now you can take us through the rest of the work-up to the op and the actions on target.'

They sailed at dawn the next day. Their stocks of fuel, food and ammunition had been replenished, the ship's crew and the black ops personnel had all been fully briefed and were ready for whatever might be thrown at them. They entered the southern end of the Suez Canal the following day. The *Al Shaheen* was once more operating under its protective camouflage, decked out from stem to stern with flags and bunting, with the crew dressed in an assortment of Middle Eastern and western clothing and blaring music through the ship's loudspeakers just like a billionaire's guests partying like there was no tomorrow.

As they motored into the Canal, watching from the bridge, Harper could see massive Egyptian military installations on both banks and he knew that as they transited through it, there would be dozens of others dotted along both banks. In bulldozer scrapes in the ground he could see a mixture of Russian and US armoured vehicles. There were Russian SA-6 mobile surface-to-air missile launchers, equipped with optical sights and radar with a continuous wave illuminator, and the successor to the SA-6, the SA-11 "Buk" self-propelled SAM launchers that could counter Cruise missiles, smart bombs, rotary wing aircraft and attack drones like Predators. He could also see SA-13s, very mobile, fast-reaction SAMs, aimed using optical and infra-red guidance, making them immune to jamming of radio-frequencies.

The Egyptians also had eight-wheeled Russian BTR personnel carriers, equipped with 14.5mm and 7.62 machine guns that could be elevated to very steep angles, making them equally effective against targets on mountain slopes, in city high-rise buildings, or against slow, low-flying air targets like helicopters. There were also the even more formidable BMPs, tracked vehicles known as "battle taxis" that were a combination of an armoured personnel carrier and a light tank. The interior was armoured and radiation-shielded and they were armed with a 73mm gun and a launcher for wire-guided, anti-tank missiles.

Although most of the equipment was Russian, Harper could also see American M-113s, the most widely used armoured vehicles in Vietnam that were called "The Green Dragons" by the Viet Cong, because they could smash through dense jungle to launch an attack. Last but by no means least in this impressive armoury was the Russian ZSU-23-4, easily identifiable by the prominent radar dish it carried. It was equipped with four 23mm auto-cannon with a rate of fire that had earned it the nickname of "the sewing machine" in Afghanistan. Well-named, Harper thought, because it could certainly stitch you up. Combining mobility, accuracy and fire power, it was the battlefield destroyer of low-flying aircraft, launching a blizzard of shells into the sky.

The drones had now been launched from the *Al Shaheen* to overfly the ship and survey the ground on either side of the Canal. The images they sent back made it possible to see the military positions and the pathways between them, indicating sentry locations, feeding and rest areas. The impression the installations gave to a casual glance was of a formidable concentration of power and menace, but when Harper ranged over them with his high-powered binoculars, he formed a different view.

He handed Laiya the binoculars. 'Take a look through those,' he said. 'You'll see that many of those military vehicles are unserviceable - they've got sand blown up around the drive-wheels, so they won't be going anywhere in a hurry and there's a general air of decay and dilapidation hanging over the whole area. My guess would be that much of the weaponry and equipment will be similarly poorly maintained and I'm not sure how much appetite the soldiers manning them would actually have for a fight if it came to it. Most of them look overweight and out of condition, their uniforms are tatty and quite a few of them are asleep.'

There were many civilians also loitering on the banks at the entrance to the Canal. Most would have been innocent enough, but among them, Harper knew, there would be eyes closely watching the comings and goings of ships. Some might only be there to alert the vendors of souvenirs that flocked around likely ships, shouting up at the decks and brandishing their goods for the tourists. Others could be spotting vessels for criminal gangs, looking for vulnerable vessels that might be boarded and robbed, or rich passengers who could be kidnapped and ransomed, but still others might be spies and look-outs for the fundamentalists operating in the deep desert where Egyptian army patrols rarely ventured and if they did, were often out-gunned.

The *Al Shaheen*'s captain had turned down the services of a pilot as they entered the Canal. He and his crew had made many transits through it before and neither they nor the black ops team had any desire to have a sharp-eyed Egyptian pilot on board, in case he caught sight of something he wasn't supposed to see, such as heavily-armed soldiers on what was purporting to be a pleasure cruise.

Shortly after passing through the entrance to the Canal, they used the on-board crane to offload a couple of dune buggies on either bank of the Canal. To maintain the cover of a pleasure cruise, the dune buggies were gaudily painted and the crew of two in each one were dressed in shirts and shorts and acting the role of spoilt rich kids on a day out. However, under their brightly coloured environmental covers, the buggies were armed with either a .50 Browning machine gun or a Milan wire-guided anti-tank missile. Harper, wrapped in voluminous Arab robes to conceal his pale, north European skin, was in one of the buggies on the north bank of the Canal, the area which he considered posed the greatest threat.

The reports received from the Saudi AWACs overflying the region, just as Harper and the other buggy crews were disembarking, had indicated suspicious communications activity in the area they were approaching. He at once thumbed the button to communicate with the other buggies. 'We need to be ready for anything and if something does happen, we will need to deal with it pretty damn quick, because the Israeli air force will be aware of the same radio signals our AWACs is intercepting and they will be ready to react to any unusual activity or loud detonation in the area, in case it is a SCUD missile or something similar targeting Israeli territory. And as you all know, the Israelis tend to shoot first and say "Halt, who goes there?" afterwards.'

There was a profusion of vehicle tracks but only the occasional paved road as the buggies began patrolling the area between the Canal and the foothills in the far distance, returning to the *Al Shaheen* occasionally to refuel the vehicles and rehydrate the crews. Even from as little as a hundred yards away, the Canal itself was lost to sight, giving them the surreal impression that the yacht was cruising through an ocean of desert sand, rather than a channel of water. The terrain was a mixture of exposed rock outcrops, hard-packed gritty sand, and soft, shifting dunes.

Harper, driving the buggy, with his crewmate sitting behind him, had just returned to the yacht to take on more fuel and water and was driving away from it again when in front of him at a distance of a couple of kilometres he saw a large cloud of dust erupt into the air. Almost at the same moment there was the shatteringly loud bang of a shell landing on the canal bank close to the *Al Shaheen*, followed by the sound of the smaller bang reaching them from the area of the dust cloud.

'Clear the Browning for action!' Harper shouted to his crewman. 'They've made the classic mistake of not damping down the area behind the gun to prevent a dust cloud, so they've given themselves away. But keep your eyes peeled for others, because they won't be hunting alone.'

The other buggy, patrolling the same bank a mile behind Harper, was also turning towards the threat. Driving at full speed to where he now knew the enemy were and laying a dust trail behind them that stretched for half a mile, Harper ordered his gunner to put down covering fire while the buggy jumped and crashed its way across the uneven ground towards the target.

Glancing over his shoulder he saw that the yacht was taking hits. Some of the bunting and flags were ablaze but it had increased speed to get out of the danger area, with the Kevlar plates in position to minimise any damage.

Looking ahead he found they were closing rapidly on what he thought were three Toyota pick-ups, one armed with a recoilless rifle, either an American M-106 or a Soviet B-10. The other two pick-ups were each armed with single ZU-23s, originally designed as anti-aircraft cannon, but which could do serious damage to ground targets too.

'Spray the general area with the '50,' Harper shouted above the roar of the engine, 'just make sure they keep their bloody heads down!'

Increasing speed still more, the buggy bucked even harder across the broken ground as they closed rapidly on their target. The crews of the pick-ups became aware too late of the buggy closing upon them. Their gunners made frantic efforts to bring their weapons to bear but they were slow to adjust and their aim was further hampered by the way the buggy was jumping around as it jolted and lurched its way towards them. Shells burst either side of the buggy, raising columns of sand and dust while shrapnel and rock splinters knifed through the air.

Realising that they were themselves now the target, the drivers of the pick-ups tried to flee, speeding off along a narrow wadi, hoping to escape into the mass of valleys in the foothills. But Harper sent his buggy roaring along the rim of the wadi, allowing his gunner to spray the fleeing convoy. As the first vehicle was hit, the Browning's shells ripped through the flimsy bodywork, even punching holes in the engine block, and sending the bloodied bodies of the driver and gunner catapulting into the desert sand. The pick-up slewed to a halt in a cloud of dust and thick oily smoke. Harper was rapidly closing on the others when there was a sudden, bowel-loosening "Crump!" sound and one of the pick-ups disappeared, vaporised in an instant, in an inferno of fire and smoke.

'What the fuck was that?' he said, his gaze raking the surroundings for the source of that destruction. He glanced up in time to see an Israeli F-15 Strike Eagle clawing its way back into the sky. 'Stop! Stop! Stop!' he shouted into his radio mic. 'Abandon the buggies and get well away from them because when the Israelis have finished dealing with the other toe-rags, I can guarantee they will sort us out as well. Repeat! Abandon the buggies, and get well away from them!'

He stamped on the brakes, bringing the buggy to a juddering halt, undid his safety harness and with his crew man alongside him, they sprinted as fast as their legs would carry them to what he hoped would be the safety of a shallow depression in the ground.

He rolled on his back but kept his face covered, because he knew from experience that even in a fast jet travelling at Mach 2 - over 1500 miles an hour - a pilot could pick up a white face from several thousand feet. After what he had already witnessed, he didn't want to become the target of the next strike. He watched a second Strike Eagle roll down and drop a couple of bombs into the wadi where the remaining pick-ups were blown to smithereens.

Everything was silent for a few seconds, and his crewman was starting to scramble to his feet when Harper shouted. 'Get down! Get down! The bastards aren't finished yet.' His words were drowned by the roar of returning fast jets and the ground-shaking blasts as the Strike Eagles used their wing mounted cannon pods to destroy Harper's buggy, reducing it to tiny shreds of metal in micro-seconds. They then turned their attention to the other buggy and after that too was destroyed, the aircraft climbed vertically back up into the clear blue sky and disappeared from sight, leaving behind them only wreckage, blood and bodies and the stench of jet fuel and cordite.

Making the after-action checks, Harper discovered that his crewman had sustained a flesh wound on his lower leg, and though he could walk, it was with great difficulty. The crew from the other buggy made their way to RV with him, and he reviewed the situation. 'We've no comms,' he said. 'They went with the buggies and we have no food and very little water. Water is probably not such a big deal to you guys, but it will be to me. We have a long hike back to the mother-ship and we have a guy with an injured leg. However, the only way out of this alive is to move at our fastest towards where we hope the *Al Shaheen* will be. The wounded guy will have to be carried because if he tries to walk, his wound will be constantly re-opening. So to summarise, we need to get a move on. I'll carry the wounded guy, because I got us into this, so it's my responsibility to get us out of it.'

They began to trek across the desert, trying to pick a way across the stonier ground where the going underfoot was easier than on the soft, shifting sand dunes. The heat was ferocious, rising in shimmering waves from the desert floor. They had only the water bottles at their belts, for the rest of their water supplies had been destroyed by the jets. Harper rationed his water, taking only a couple of sips at a time, and then forcing himself to walk at least a mile before another sip. The water did little more than briefly moisten his mouth and his thirst grew more and more intense, while the pounding headache that was increasing as he became ever more dehydrated only added to his discomfort. He forced himself to focus only on the ground ahead, ignoring the weight of his crewman, carried in a fireman's lift across his shoulder.

After a gut-busting few hours, plodding through the desert, Harper thought he glimpsed movement ahead, but he could not be sure, afraid it was just another of the wavering images and mirages created by the heat. However after trudging a little further, he heard the sound of an engine note and a moment later a buggy came into view and sped towards them. One of the other two buggies had been trans-shipped across the canal from the other bank and had been patrolling, looking for Harper and his group. 'We'd almost given up hope of finding you,' the driver said.

'You and me both,' Harper said. He allowed them to lift his now unconscious crewman from his shoulders and then sank to his knees, letting relief wash over him. He drained the rest of his water in one gulp, but insisted on waiting until the injured crewman and the others had been ferried back to the Al Shaheen in relays, before climbing into the buggy himself. Without any further dramas, a short while later he was languishing in the VIP quarters of the yacht being rehydrated with the finest iced water money could buy.

Laiya gave him a quizzical look. 'All right?'

He nodded. 'It was a bit hairy for a while but it was a good learning curve. We dished out some dirt, we took some dirt, we got away with only a flesh wound and most importantly, nobody was left behind.'

Chapter 10

The *Al Shaheen* cleared the northern end of the Suez Canal that evening and set a course to the west. The propulsion jets drove the ship at a steady forty knots, but even at that speed it took thirty hours to reach Malta, 1500 miles away. The ship's crew spent the time in transit from the Canal cleaning up the damage from the enemy action, most of which was superficial and required little more than a coat of paint.

Meanwhile Lex had called a Council of War with Laiya, Saif and the Saudi black ops team to finalise the plans for the next phase of the operation. He had already noted a positive change in the Saudis. With their new-found confidence after their recent combat experiences, they were a different group to the guys who had been assembled at the start of the mission. Harper had mentioned this to Laiya. 'They remind me of my days in the Paras,' he said 'because while the other regiments just marched, the Paras marched with a swagger because they knew they were the best. I get the same feeling from your guys now.'

Maintaining the cover of being a billionaire's party boat, the yacht was now once more rigged with flags from stem to stern, with music blaring and a light show on board at night. When the *Al Shaheen*'s captain brought the ship to anchor in the middle of Valletta's Grand Harbour, he kept it well away from the jetties and he kept the landing stage raised to avoid unwanted visitors, but they were still inundated with uninvited would-be guests, heading out to the ship in small boats and water taxis and trying, without success, to blag their way on board. When any of the crew ventured ashore, they were mobbed by local traders and surrounded by women from Valletta's notorious Gut - the red light district that had been catering to passing sailors since the heyday of the British Empire.

The *Al Shaheen*'s tender was tied up alongside a jetty at the harbourside. It was crewed by a couple of very smart sailors, who were looking around curiously, trying to spot the passenger they were expecting - the member of Harper's team flying in from the UK. They were intrigued to see what this new guy would look like, and how they might measure up against him. What they did not expect was the small nondescript-looking individual who emerged from the crowd of spectators, carrying an overnight bag and a computer carrier over his shoulders. The man wore gloves despite the heat of the day.

Stepping clumsily aboard the tender, he nodded towards the yacht and said 'Okay, let's go, I'm the guy you've been waiting for.'

Arriving on the bridge of the ship he was greeted warmly by Harper who, after a welcoming hug, introduced him to Laiya and Saif, as ever in close attendance. 'Allow me to introduce my good friend Hansfree.'

Laiya embarrassed herself by letting her surprise show when she shook hands with him and found that his hand was a rubber prosthetic.

Hansfree just smiled 'Don't worry, it's a surprise to everyone I meet. And do you know what's even more surprising?' He held up his other hand. 'I've got another one just like it. An IED was the cause, in case you were wondering.'

Within minutes of his arrival the yacht was being readied for sea and Hansfree was deep in conversation with Harper and Laiya, while simultaneously readying his computer for the coming action.

'Right,' Harper said. 'We needed you here in advance, but we must also get the rest of the usual team to Belgrade ASAP.'

'I gave Barry Big and Barry Whisper a heads up and they are both ready and waiting,' Hansfree said, 'but Maggie May won't be available for this one, Lex. Her son isn't well and she doesn't want to leave him.'

'So we'll need a replacement for Maggie May on this op, and it's probably best if it's another woman.' He thought for a moment. 'I reckon we'll go for Annie Laurie.'

Harper had known Annie for just three years but he was impressed with her. Her father was an

Intelligence Liaison Officer with the SAS in Northern Ireland. He was also an alcoholic and was killed in a road traffic accident when he drove off the road while returning, drunk, from a meeting with the RUC Special Branch. At the time Annie was still a young teenager, living in North-East Scotland, studying hard and determined to have a career in IT. However she had been devoted to her father, and as a result of his death, she made a swift mental career change. As soon as she was able, she left school and joined the Royal Air Force. Through that unusual route, by the time she was nineteen she had applied for and been successful in joining 14 Int. She did a decent stint with them but eventually got disillusioned and quit. She found work on the Circuit - the unofficial network of former Paras, Special Forces and 14 Int operatives that shares news of jobs in everything from security and body guarding to mercenary soldiering and other, even darker occupations.

'Good call,' said Hansfree. 'She's a pro.'

The *Al Shaheen*'s course from Malta took it through the straits between the "heel" of Italy and Albania into the Adriatic, and eventually they anchored off Dubrovnik, a tourist honeypot where several other luxury yachts were already berthed.

'We'll use the on-board heli to transfer to the airport just outside Belgrade,' Laiya said. 'The heli is a Bell 525, so it has a large enough payload and enough speed to do the trip, overflying Bosnia-Herzegovina and Western Serbia in about an hour.'

'Sounds good,' Harper said, 'but when we get to the airport and the hotel you will have to act a role. Can you play the part of a diva Princess?'

'Play it? I know how to be a Princess - I am one - so I only need to play at being a diva.' She paused and gave Harper a smile that raised his pulse a few notches. 'Unless you think I'm already one of those too.'

He glanced at Saif, who as usual was fingering the silken rope at his waist. 'I've not seen any evidence of that so far, but I'll be watching closely to see how natural the performance looks when we get to Belgrade.'

She laughed. 'Then I must be sure not to disappoint you.'

When they arrived at Belgrade airport in the ship's helicopter, the Princess immediately began to cause chaos. They had brought dozens of Louis Vuitton suitcases and half a dozen steamer trunks with them and at once Laiya began imperiously ordering everyone about, while handing out lavish US dollar tips to anyone who could get close enough to grab one. Porters were sent scurrying left and right under the mountains of luggage, while she completely ignored the immigration officials and just kept saying in bad English 'diplomatic', and then showing a sheaf of papers covered in Arabic script. She repeated the performance with the customs officials, then marched straight out of the airport followed by her entourage of Saif, Harper, Hansfree and the Saudi black ops team.

Not one of them had had their passport checked as they followed in her wake into the fleet of hired limousines awaiting them and sped away from the airport.

'So far so good,' Harper said as he settled back in his seat. 'an absolutely convincing performance, Princess, you're either a natural or you've been typecast! That's got the weaponry and the operations kit through customs, a repeat performance at the hotel will see us in fine shape.'

When they arrived at the five star Square Nine Hotel in the heart of the Old Town of Belgrade, there was no attempt to make a discreet arrival. Laiya was once more in her element, scattering hotel guests like chaff as she strode through the lobby, barking orders at any hotel staff who crossed her path, and dispensing tips left, right and centre. Their cover was that they were a Saudi delegation in Belgrade to discuss investment opportunities in Serbia, though in fact the only investment they would be discussing was the purchase of a tactical nuclear device from the Serbian mafiosi.

Soon they were making themselves comfortable in the top floor suites of the hotel with the staff, already well lubricated with eye-watering tips, on full alert to provide any service asked of them in the hope of collecting further lavish rewards.

The other members of Harper's own support team - Barry Big, Barry Whisper and Annie Laurie - had already arrived and they met with him, Laiya and the rest of the team for a briefing in the Presidential Suite that Laiya had taken. Once Hansfree had swept the room for bugs - 'Those old Soviet habits die hard,' he said, as he removed a listening device from the overhead light and another from the room telephone, Harper introduced the surveillance team to Laiya and then briefed them.

'There are three main areas of interest. One is obviously here, since the hotel where the Saudi delegation is staying will draw interested spectators of all sorts like flies round shit. The other two areas of interest are the airport and the as yet undecided hand-over point for the device. As you know it is easier to spot surveillance from the outside so I need to know from you who is in town, whether it is just Serbians, or any combination of Serbians, Russians and Iranians. We will be flying a Saudi C-130 into the airport to make a simulated delivery of the payment for the Tac Nuke. In reality there are already more than enough US dollars on board the *Al Shaheen* to pay any amount Laiya might be asked for, but it'll be helpful to put on a bit of a show to flush out any watchers - and I expect there to be plenty of them. If you concentrate surveillance in the first instance on the hotel and the airport, any spare time you can find can then be spent on reconnaissance of a place for the hand-over. We are looking for a hollow in a quiet rural area, something shaped like an amphitheatre, where the buyers and sellers can meet away from prying eyes and outside interference.'

'I'll do a Google Earth search,' said Hansfree. 'I should be able to give them a steer.'

Harper nodded. 'When we get to the hand-over stage later on, it's likely that we will need to set up a Rural OP. Any kit they need can be bought locally. A lot of the local shops will sell foldable saws, chicken wire and secateurs, but they may need a couple of square yards of camouflage netting each, which probably won't be as easy to source locally. If we have any issues with that, we can bring it in from the *Al Shaheen*.'

The surveillance team set to work at once and were soon relaying an almost constant stream of information back to Hansfree, who was running the comms and electronic surveillance from another suite at the hotel. Working under the cover story of being a British nanny looking for high-end clients, Annie Laurie was able to visit all of the top end hotels in the city several times. She tipped the concierge at each hotel a few dollars, asking him to keep an eye out for any guests who might have need of her services as a temporary nanny or babysitter. However, had anyone been watching her closely, they might have noticed that as she sat in the lobby sipping a coffee, her focus was not on any guests with children, but any bulky male figures who passed through.

Barry Big had meanwhile reinvented himself as an air cargo executive, carrying out hangar surveys and touting for new business, which gave him ample excuse to spend his time in and around the airport. Barry Whisper was passing himself off as a holidaymaker, taking in the tourist sights around the city centre. They missed little or nothing that went on in their respective jurisdictions and before long Hansfree was handing Laiya and Harper a dossier of sightings.

Annie Laurie said that 'rough-looking types', some with suspicious bulges under their armpits or in the waistband at the back of their trousers, under their jackets, had been visiting the Square Nine hotel. They had been drinking in the lobby and had also tried to blag or bribe their way up to the executive floors where the Saudi delegation was staying, though so far they had been unsuccessful. Barry Big reported that the airport area had been staked out by a 'foreign-looking' team using a couple of minibuses. Barry Whisper added that there were also 'a few Middle Eastern types, possibly Iranians, floating around the city centre and watching the hotel.

After discussing it with Laiya, Harper decided it was time to bring in the C-130 to flush out the various factions. Hansfree then started rumours in various internet chatrooms that a US military team was arriving in Belgrade to carry out the arrest of a Serbian war criminal who had been in hiding since the end of the Bosnian war over twenty years before. As a result Serbian reporters and TV news crews descended on the airport in droves, and when the military Hercules landed and taxied over to the General Aviation area there was a flurry of excitement, with reporters and cameramen sprinting to secure vantage points and then beginning to file reports about the mystery aircraft that were soon filling the Serbian airwaves.

The Bell 525 helicopter, its engine running, was already parked on the apron, when the ramp of the C-130 opened and a squad of armed Saudi infantrymen descended and fanned out to surround the Herc and the helicopter. Another squad then came down the aircraft ramp, staggering under the apparent weight of a heavy timber box they carried from the cargo hold of the aircraft, placing it inside the 525. Immediately, the engines revved up, the rotors accelerated to a blur and within a few seconds the heli was flying south-west away from the airport. The Saudi soldiers climbed back aboard the Hercules and it lost no time in taking off and disappearing due east.

The news crews hadn't got quite the story they were expecting but they had something to show for their efforts and the coverage produced a reaction from the different factions. Hansfree intercepted a flurry of internet, phone and radio chatter, as the various teams reported to their bosses, and their increased activity around the Square Nine hotel, as they tried to establish what the Saudis were up to, enabled Harper's surveillance team to make definite identifications of the nationality of the various factions.

There were definitely three of them. The Middle Eastern types, 95 per cent certain to be Iranians, were staying in another upmarket hotel in the city centre, while the Serbian and Russian mafiosi were based in the same Gasthaus in the Old Town, just a couple of blocks from the Square Nine.

Having established who they were facing, Harper told the surveillance team to head out of the city and locate a satisfactory site for the hand-over of the money and Tac Nuke, once Laiya had completed the deal.

'We know what and who we are up against now,' he said to Laiya, 'so now we just need to dispense with the go-between you've been using - pay him off with whatever it takes to get rid of him - so that you can negotiate the final price direct with the Serbs. I can't negotiate for you, because I don't know what your final price is and also the sight of a non-Saudi facing them might make the Serbians smell a rat. But the sight of a Brit acting as bodyguard to a wealthy and powerful Saudi is not exactly unusual, so that's the role I'll be playing. You'll have to do the deal yourself but I and the rest of your team will be right behind you, at your shoulder.'

The meeting with the Serbs took place on the forecourt of what had once been a car-showroom but was now just another empty and derelict industrial building in a rust-belt district of the city. Harper's team had had the place under observation since the previous day and while Laiya, Saif, Harper and four of her black ops team waited in the open to greet the Serbs when they arrived, Barry Big and the other eight Saudis were all watching from cover, ready to make an armed intervention if the meeting turned ugly. The Serbs rolled up in two black 4x4s with a two-man negotiating team flanked by six bodyguards, who were near-identical hulking figures, all equipped with mirrored sunglasses and scowling expressions.

Harper could hear Barry Big's voice in his earpiece. 'They look just like nightclub bouncers.'

Harper hid a smile. 'They probably are, but not of any club that I'd want to be visiting.'

While the Serb bodyguards and Laiya's back-up team eyed each other suspiciously, their principals got down to the negotiations. The wrangling went on for over half an hour and Harper didn't need to be able to overhear what they were saying to recognise that there was a big gap between what Laiya was offering and what the Serbs were demanding.

'Bloody hell, there's more hand-waving, head-shaking and finger-wagging than an Italian football team disputing a penalty,' Barry Big said.

'Careful BB,' Harper muttered into his throat mic. 'Your prejudices are showing.'

At one point Laiya even shrugged and turned away as if about to walk off to her car, but the Serbs called her back and negotiations resumed. Eventually, after one last heated exchange, the Serb's chief negotiator spread his hands wide and then nodded and shook Laiya's hand.

'Looks like job done,' Harper said, 'but let's not relax our vigilance until the Serbs have cleared the area.'

The rest waited until the black 4x4s had pulled out and driven off back towards the centre of Belgrade before emerging from cover.

'Nice bit of brinkmanship there, Laiya,' Harper said. 'I thought at one point it was game over.'

'So did I,' she said, 'but I held my nerve and in the end they gave in. They kept telling me the Iranians had promised to match any figure we offered, but I told them that the Iranians could promise whatever they liked but only we Saudis had the cash to make good on our promises. So we've agreed the deal and the hand-over of the Tac Nuke will take place in three days' time at a site that we will specify to them.'

'But we can't expect the Iranians to just lie back and accept it,' Harper said. 'So we'll need to keep a close eye on them in case they try to pull anything before the hand-over or when we're doing it.' He gave a brisk nod. 'Right, I'll be leaving you for 24 hours. My surveillance team has identified a number of potential places for the hand-over, so I need to go and check them out. I'll give you the co-ordinates as soon as we've decided on the place and then you can finalise the arrangements with the Serbs. Tell them the rules of the hand-over will be One - everyone attending will be unarmed. Two - we will arrive first, followed by the Serbs, who will bring the device with them. Three - we will check that it is genuine and then, and only then, will the money be delivered. Four, the cash will be dropped from our helicopter, and once the Serbs have checked it and are happy.

Five - they will depart the hand-over place first and we will follow. If the Serbs try to alter any of these details, be prepared to walk. If you're hard-nosed about it, they will fall into line, but if we deviate from the plan, we could end up coming to serious harm.'

She gave him a sceptical look. 'Do you really think the Serbs will turn up unarmed?'

'No, of course not, but we need to give them a false sense of security, while still doing things our way.'

Harper returned to the hotel briefly and was then able to slip out again, hefting a heavy sports bag. After carrying out intricate anti-surveillance manoeuvres, he rendezvoused with the rest of his team. They were driving a rented 4 x 4 and after further anti-surveillance drills, they were soon in rural south-west Serbia, a sparsely populated area of low, round-shouldered mountains and broad valleys.

With infinite patience, they checked out each of the locations identified by Hansfree from Google Earth and then evaluated by the rest of the surveillance team. Harper found flaws with either the location or the lay-out of each of the first four selected areas but finally, he pronounced himself happy with the fifth site they visited. It was a disused and overgrown quarry, with a vertical wall on one side and steep but negotiable scrubby slopes on the other sides, a bit reminiscent of the Roman amphitheatres which dotted the Adriatic coast. Around the top of the quarry there was a tangle of brambles and other thorn bushes, and over the whole area neither Harper nor the others could find any trace of recent human activity, just the tracks of animals.

Harper, Barry Big, Barry Whisper and Annie Laurie then had an intense discussion on the various scenarios that might play out and the best means of dealing with each of them. They then spent a long time measuring angles, ranges and distances before Harper pronounced himself satisfied. He offered to take them back to Belgrade until nearer the time of the hand-over but was not surprised when Annie Laurie shook her head. 'No, we'll stick it out here, won't we guys? We need to be absolutely one hundred per cent certain that we are not going to be disturbed by dog walkers or bird-watchers when the hand-over is taking place. That way we'll be ready to go whenever you pull the pin.'

'All right,' Harper said. 'Now we've specified to the Serbs that they must come unarmed. They'll ignore that, of course, and when this kicks off, I reckon they will come armed with Makarov semi-automatics. The later Russian SF weapons are based on the AK family and are too big to conceal, but the Makarovs are easy to hide. But I would bet the farm that some of them will also be bringing Skorpion VZ-61 machine pistols. They are readily available on the black market here, are not much bigger than the Makarov and so just as easy to hide but, firing 850 rounds a minute on fully automatic, they pack a whole lot more punch.'

He unzipped the hefty sports bag he had brought with him and showed them the contents. 'To counter those, I've brought you each an M-16 with an Alpha Charlie Oscar Golf: the US Advanced Combat Optical Gunsight. The Saudis like them but with the short ranges we're going to be working over you'll need to decide for yourselves whether to use them or not. There will be no opportunity to zero the weapons so if you do fire, go for a body shot.'

While Harper double-checked the co-ordinates of the site and then set off back to Belgrade, Annie Laurie, Barry Big and Barry Whisper began setting up their OPs. Building an OP was something that came as naturally as breathing to ex-members of 14 Int. In urban areas, they would choose a room in an abandoned building, a skip, a pile of rubble or even a roof-void in an occupied house. While the house-owners, completely unaware of the intruders in their midst, blithely carried on with their normal lives, over their heads the surveillance team would have moved in, removed a slate from the roof to give them a view of the target building and then they would remain there for as long as it took to gather the necessary intelligence - sometimes weeks. They would then leave as discreetly as they arrived, and everything that they had brought in with them, food and water containers, even urine and excrement, would be taken away with them in sealed plastic bags, leaving no visible trace behind that they had ever been there.

Rural OPs, like the ones they were setting up in the quarry in south-west Serbia, required a different approach. They began by selecting a suitable bush or a patch of undergrowth. Thorn bushes were preferred because these were routinely avoided by humans and animals. Before starting to build the OP, the operator would check for animal tracks surrounding it. Badgers were always best avoided because they could be aggressive, especially when protecting young, and nesting birds were also bad news because they would make a prodigious racket to try to get the operator to move, possibly alerting hostile forces in the area.

Having found the right bush, the operator began by making a single vertical cut on the outside of the bush on the opposite side to the target. He then wriggled into the bush, cutting further stems and branches as he went. Once he was fully inside the bush, still lying prone, he turned over and, lying on his back, he began to cut upwards and sideways to achieve the desired dome shape right in the heart of the bush.

Once he had cut the inside to the desired dimensions, if necessary he would support the bush by using chicken wire to hold it in its original shape, and inside this he tied pieces of camouflage netting to prevent light from penetrating into the centre of the bush. The severed vegetation would die but it would take a few days before it became obvious - long enough for the job in hand.

Once the operator was happy with his angles of view to the target, he brought in all his operational gear, and then sealed the entrance to his hide by tying the branches flanking the entrance cut together with wire. Finally, he got a third party - sometimes one of the other operators and sometimes a person brought in specifically to do that task - to view the OP from a distance to make absolutely sure that nothing had been missed that might give the OP away.

Very good operators would not leave their OP at all during daylight, taking small sips of water and eating hard rations, until night-time when they might leave the OP and move a short distance away to relieve themselves, do some exercises and possibly have a warm drink before returning to the OP well before first light. Excellent operators - and Barry Big, Barry Whisper and Annie Laurie were the best you could get - would not leave their OP at all, taking minimum liquid and solid refreshment, and relieving themselves when necessary into plastic bags which they would take back to base for disposal at the end of the operation. To prevent cramp, these operators had their own programmes of calisthenics, usually the clenching and unclenching of muscles in various parts of the body.

The day before the hand-over was due to take place, Harper and Laiya held a final briefing on the op. 'We can expect the Serbs to turn up a couple of hours ahead of the scheduled time,' Harper said. 'So I'll make sure that I and the team are in place several hours before that.'

'I?' Laiya said. 'You mean we don't you? I've not come along on this operation just to sit in the background doing my needlework like a demure housewife, while the men go out and do the real work. This is my operation and my men, so I will be leading them.'

'With respect, Laiya, you've done a great job getting us to this point but this is where the shot and shell might start flying if anything goes wrong,' said Harper. 'And if it does, I need a team of people who are combat-ready.'

'And I'm as combat-ready as any of my men. I need to be part of this operation.'

'And you are,' said Harper.

'No, I need to be at the cutting edge, not sitting back at base.' She glared at him. 'You don't respect me and nor do my men.'

From the corner of his eye, Harper could see Saif, responding to her anger, half-rising to his feet, as his hand inevitably strayed to the silk rope at his waist.

'I'm as skilled as any of my men,' Laiya said. 'I'm as good a shot as any of them, and I'm as fit and as fast as them, but it's still not enough. I need to show them - to show you - that I'm not just their equal but I'm better than them. I know I can do it but I want my men to know it too. I see the way some of them look at me and talk behind their hands. They think I'm a princess in every sense, and only got this job because of who I am and who I'm related to, not what I can do. If they said it to my face, I'd stuff their words down their throats, but they never do, though I know they're thinking it.'

'I don't do requests, Laiya,' Harper said. 'And I choose my teams on merit. The aim is to get the result so we need the people who are best-qualified, trained and equipped to achieve that result. Is that you?'

'Yes it is. I'm as fit as any of my men, I'm in the top ten per cent of every firing test and I'm a woman and that alone might make a Serbian gangster hesitate for half a second before pulling the trigger - long enough for me to make the killing shot myself. So, I'm not some princess who needs a man to protect her.'

'All right, calm down, I surrender, you've convinced me. You're on the team for the hand-over but if the shooting starts, there can be no favours, and god help me if you get hit and I have to explain that to Saif, let alone Anwar.'

'It's my decision and my responsibility,' she said.

When the briefing was over, Harper slipped away from the others and placed a call on a secure phone Hansfree had given him. He spoke swiftly and urgently, his voice low. If the Saudis were up to their jobs, they would detect that a call had been made but they would not be able to decipher its content, and if they traced it to Harper and chose to interrogate him about it, he had a plausible cover story in place.

In the half-light of dawn the next morning, Harper, Laiya, Saif and the other Saudis made their way by torchlight from the lip of the quarry down the slope to the foot of the cliff.

'I didn't see your surveillance team,' Laiya said.

'You weren't supposed to. They're doing what they are being paid to do. I intended to do this part on my own but you invited yourself along. However, you have got to do things my way. If I tell you to do something, I don't want a discussion, I just want action, all right?'

She nodded but couldn't hide a smile. 'Of course, I will be as demure as a Muslim bride.'

'That I don't believe. Now, when the Serbs come, with or without their Russian allies, I expect them to be armed and I also expect them to be followed by the Iranians, because they have been following them ever since this began. I don't think the Serbs have the wit to realise that, nor do I think the Iranians will just pack up and go home without an attempt to hijack the proceedings and grab the Tac Nuke for themselves.'

At his direction, the majority of the Saudis spread themselves around the quarry, going to ground in positions from where they could give cover to Harper, Laiya and Saif, but also return fire if an attack was launched from any part of the quarry.

As Harper had predicted, over ninety minutes before the scheduled hand-over time, they heard the sound of approaching vehicles and shortly afterwards there was a crashing in the bushes above them as a group of eight Serbs stumbled down the slope towards them, with a couple of them carrying large back packs which they dropped on the ground in front of Laiya.

'There is the device, check it, bring the money and then we can get out of here,' the Serbian leader said.

'I thought we agreed that there would only be three of you,' Laiya said. 'But now we are here, we may as well continue. Lex, check it out.'

Harper opened up the back packs and quickly examined the contents. 'They look genuine, so by all means go ahead and pay the man.'

Laiya thumbed her radio and moments later they heard the thunder of helicopter rotors, rapidly growing louder as it approached. Under the cover of the noise and the clouds of dust caused by the heli as it descended towards the quarry floor, a further group of armed men - the Iranians who had been tracking the Serbs for days - had appeared on the rim of the quarry. When the heli was about ten feet from the ground, a crewman kicked out a wooden box which hit the ground with a thump as the helicopter climbed steeply away. It was only then that the groups at the bottom of the quarry became aware of the armed men at the top.

Immediately the Serbs and Russians pulled out their concealed pistols and Skorpions and began shooting at the men on the rim of the quarry, but their rounds were falling short because of the range, whereas the AK-47 rounds of the Iranians were now smacking into the dust around them and striking sparks and splinters from the rocks. Rounds and ricochets filled the air for a moment but then there was a fresh burst of firing, this time from the M-16s of

Barry Big, Barry Whisper and Annie Laurie, hidden in their OPs and unseen by anyone until they opened fire. A split-second later Laiya's black ops team members began opening up from their positions as well and the Iranians were cut apart in the crossfire. One by one they plummeted down the quarry face or tumbled down into the scrub, dead before they hit the ground.

Still in cover, the Saudi black ops team had now trained their weapons on the Serbs, but held their fire for fear of hitting Laiya, Harper and Saif. Harper saw the Serb leader exchange a glance with one of his men, and then began to swing his gun barrel towards Laiya. She had spotted the movement as well and made a grab for the weapon, but he side-stepped her, and then pistol-whipped her across the jaw. With a scream of rage, Saif hurled himself at him but was taken down by a single shot to the chest from one of the Serb's henchmen.

The firing had triggered a small rockfall on the cliffs behind them, and that momentary distraction was all Harper needed. He smashed the heel of his hand upwards at the nearest Serb's nose, driving a splinter of bone up into the brain and killing him instantly. Even as the Serb was falling, Harper had snatched the Skorpion machine pistol from his lifeless hand, brought it to bear on the others and began taking them down, the rounds punching holes in their chests and exiting through their backs, taking most of their heart and lungs with them. However, even in semi-automatic mode, the Scorpion had such a high rate of fire that he found it difficult to restrict his shots to double-taps and was increasingly conscious that he had at most twenty rounds in the magazine to deal with all the Serbs.

Still on the ground, Laiya squirmed across the quarry floor and snatched up a Makarov that one of the Serbs had let fall as Harper shot him. In one movement, she swung the Makarov up and shot the Serb leader in the throat, a heartbeat before he fired his own weapon at her. Harper put two more rounds into him while the sound of the first was still reverberating and the Serb fell stone dead. The rest of the Serbs were scrambling for cover, but Harper's team and the Saudis were now able to isolate targets, and the remaining Serbs were all soon dead or dying.

Yelling to the Saudis to put a double-tap into each of the fallen Serbs to make sure they were dead, Harper dropped to his knees alongside Saif and made a rapid check of his wound. He snatched a shell dressing from his belt and pressed it onto Saif's chest, slowing the blood flow. 'Saif!' he shouted, then raised his voice as he saw Saif's eyes flickering shut. 'Saif, stay with me! You need to keep up the pressure on the dressing while I call for a casevac. You're all right. You are going to make it. And you did good, Laiya is OK.'

He hit his comms and called the chopper back in. It had been lurking out of sight and earshot, just over the horizon, and within two minutes it was settling on the quarry floor in a cloud of dust. The pilot kept the rotors turning as Harper carried Saif to the chopper and then shouted at Laiya, who was sitting up with a dazed look on her face and an ugly gash on her jaw and cheek where the Serb's pistol had whipped her. 'Get on the chopper! You need treatment, pronto,' Harper said. 'And Saif will bleed out if we don't get him back to the *Al Shaheen* at once. Go back with him, then send the chopper back for the rest of us.'

She hesitated a moment, looking as if she might argue, but Harper simply grabbed her arm, dragged her to the chopper and pushed her aboard, shouting 'Go! Go! Go!' to the loadmaster as he did so.

The noise of the rotors increased to a scream as the chopper rose from the ground. It cleared the rim of the quarry within seconds, and then swung away to the west, heading for the sea where the *Al Shaheen* was waiting with the medical team already on standby.

The heli returned an hour later and Harper ordered the rest of the Saudis to go back on it, telling the pilot to return once more for him and his own team. As soon as the noise of the heli faded, they sprang into action. He took his secure phone inside his jacket, made a two second call and then, with the help of Barry Big, he began removing a part from each of the two halves of the Tac Nuke device. The two men then carried the parts of the Tac Nuke they had removed up the steep slope to the rim of the quarry.

Breathing heavily from the exertion, they were waiting for no more than five minutes before a truck appeared, bouncing and jolting along the rough track the Serb and Iranian vehicles had taken. The truck driver and his mate jumped down and then they swung the rear doors open. The truck was already almost fully loaded with disassembled steel machinery, but a narrow walkway had been left at one side. The truck driver and his mate carried the parts of the Tac Nuke that Harper and Barry Big had given him to the end of the truck and then rearranged the rest of the load as they moved slowly back, blocking the walkway they'd used. They then handed Harper and Barry Big two apparently identical parts to the ones they'd stripped from the Tac Nuke.

'Thanks,' Harper said with a smile. 'Fair exchange is no robbery.'

The driver picked up a five gallon jerry-can that was full of used engine oil and poured it all over the stacked machinery in the truck. He winked at Harper. 'Any customs man who wants to make a full inspection is going to need a new uniform afterwards, so I'm guessing they'll just look at the bill of lading and not go any further.'

They shut the doors again, locked them and fixed a carefully forged customs seal to them. The driver grinned. 'See? Already inspected and sealed anyway.' The two men got back in the cab, and roared off again, back the way they had come.

While Harper and Barry Big carried the new parts back down to the quarry floor and carefully reassembled the Tac Nuke, Barry Whisper and Annie Laurie drove all but one of the Serb and Iranian 4x4s right to the edge of the sheer cliff on the other side of the quarry, then climbed out of them, released the handbrakes and pushed them in turn over the edge. They smashed down onto the quarry floor, disintegrating into heaps of twisted metal.

Barry Whisper and Annie Laurie joined Harper and Barry Big on the quarry floor, still with a few minutes to spare before the *Al Shaheen*'s heli was due to return. When he'd finished with the Tac Nuke, Harper retrieved the pack of money that Laiya had given the Serbs and took a bundle of 500 euro notes from it. He riffled through them and then handed most of them to Barry Big. 'That's about half a million euros,' he said. 'So it should be enough for any eventuality.'

He pulled the wrappers from a couple of the other wads of money and threw them up into the air. They drifted down on the breeze, landing in the dust and among the surrounding scrub and bushes. He nodded to himself and then glanced at his watch. 'Okay, you guys need to make yourselves scarce. The heli is due back in ten minutes. And as ever, thanks for everything. Your fees will all be in the usual accounts by the time you get home. Oh and I need to fire a couple more rounds, so don't panic when you hear the shooting!'

As they made their way back up the slope, Harper laid the money-pack on the ground, picked up one of the Serb weapons and fired two rounds at close-range into it. Shreds of paper flew like thistle down as the rounds punched a fist-sized hole through the money. He examined the pack then muttered 'One more for luck' and put another round into it, causing a fresh blizzard of shredded paper.

As the echoes faded, he saw Barry Big and the others outlined on the rim of the quarry for a moment as they all raised a hand in farewell and a few seconds later he heard the sound of an engine as they drove off in the last Serb 4x4.

Harper spent the few remaining minutes while he was waiting for the returning heli in gathering up the Serbs' Makarovs and Skorpions. If the Serbian mafia sent men to search for their missing comrades, there was no sense in leaving the weapons for them to find. The dead Serbs and Iranians were left for the vultures.

He sat down on a rock to wait and within a couple of minutes he heard the sound of rotors and saw the heli sweep into view. It landed in the familiar cloud of dust, though this time it also whipped up the banknotes that Harper had scattered into a snow-storm. The loadmaster jumped down and helped him to load the Tac Nuke, the money pack and the weapons into the cargo bay, and then the heli was airborne again, and soon exited Serbian airspace for the final time. When the heli had crossed the coast of

Bosnia-Herzegovina and passed out of sight of land on its way back to the *Al Shaheen*, Harper walked to the loading bay door and dropped the Makarovs and Skorpions into the sea.

The captain of the *Al Shaheen*, a Saudi general and two military scientists were waiting on the deck as the helicopter went into a hover and then landed on the heli-pad. The captain at once took charge of the money pack, though he winced at the bullet-riddled state of it. When the loadmaster had overseen the unloading of the Tac Nuke, the general took charge of it and, ordering two sailors to carry it below decks, he hurried after them with the scientists at his heels.

Harper headed straight for the sick bay to check on Saif and Laiya. Saif was still in the operating theatre, with the surgeons working to repair his collapsed lung and the trauma and blood loss caused by the round that had hit his chest, but the prognosis for a full recovery was apparently good.

Laiya had a row of steri-strips across the gash on her face and the beginnings of a purpling bruise on her jaw but she brushed aside Harper's expressions of sympathy. 'It's nothing,' she said. 'The surgeon says it'll leave only the very faintest of scars when it's healed. So the only lasting damage will be to my pride because I let that Serb bastard side-swipe me.'

'True,' Harper said, 'but on a positive note, you did shoot him in the throat a second or two later.'

She laughed. 'Be sure to mention that in the debrief, just in case any of my men missed it.'

Towards the end of the briefing, he became aware of the *Al Shaheen*'s captain pacing up and down outside the briefing room, and as soon as it ended, he hurried into the room and held a muttered consultation with Laiya. Harper noticed that the captain glanced across at him several times as he was talking to Laiya and having expected that this would happen, he strolled over to them. 'Problems?' he said.

'Perhaps,' Laiya said, turning to face him. 'The captain tells me that it appears that some of the money is missing. Though it is difficult to be certain, since the money pack had been hit by several rounds.'

Harper kept his face expressionless. 'Really? How much?'

'Perhaps as much as half a million euros might be missing.'

Harper gave a low whistle. 'That is a lot. I didn't have the money under observation all the time while I was waiting for the heli to come back, because I was gathering up the Serbs' and Iranians weapons for disposal and pushing their vehicles over the edge of the quarry.' He shrugged. 'So there was certainly time enough when it was out of my sight for someone to sneak in and steal the money, but that seems pretty unlikely. I would stake my life on the honesty of my team and the Serbs and Iranians were all dead and in no position to help themselves to it. So unless some goat-herder or other random stranger managed to get in and out of the quarry without being seen - and that is vanishingly unlikely - I'd suggest it was either destroyed by gunfire or spilled out of the pack when the rounds hit it. There was certainly a snowstorm of banknotes when the heli landed - just ask the pilot - and we didn't stop to pick them up.'

The captain gave him a suspicious look. 'It would be quite a snowstorm, wouldn't it?'

Harper stared him down, keeping his expression neutral and his voice calm but icy cold. 'If you're suggesting that I've stolen the money, you're welcome to search me and my quarters.'

'No one is suggesting that,' Laiya said hurriedly with a warning look to the captain. 'It's just curious, that's all.'

Harper spread his hands wide. 'Well, you never told me how much your government was going to pay, but from the weight of that pack, I'd say it must have been close to ten million euros. So look at it this way: this morning your government was expecting to be ten million euros poorer by now, in exchange for that Tac Nuke. Well now, they've got nine and a half million euros back again and they've got the Tac Nuke as well. Sounds like a pretty good result to me.'

The captain compressed his lips into a thin line but said nothing and after studying Harper's expression for a few more moments, Laiya shrugged. 'Perhaps you're right, Lex, though there is one more thing. The weapons scientists can't be sure until they've carried out a full evaluation of the device, but they have raised a concern that it may have been tampered with and may not be viable.'

'Well, if so, that's not something you can lay at my door,' Harper said. 'Unless you're suggesting I had a nuclear weapons tool kit in my back pocket. If that is the case, then the Serbs must have pulled a fast one on us.'

'And yet you vouched for the fact that it was genuine,' Laiya said.

'No, I vouched for the fact that it looked genuine, just like the ones I'd seen when serving with the Paras. But I'm not a weapons scientist and since your own weapons scientists aren't sure if it's genuine or not without further tests, then any tampering, if it did happen, must have been too subtle for a common ex-soldier like me to be expected to spot.'

He nodded curtly and went up on deck. Laiya sought him out a little later. 'I'm sorry that we had to confront you about the money, Lex, but you must admit it did look suspicious. Personally I don't care what happened to the money. As you said, we got a very good result at a much lower price than we were expecting to pay, so as far as I'm concerned, it's all forgotten. Okay?'

He nodded. 'Okay.'

When Harper next checked the email drafts folder he used for communications with Charlotte Button, there was a single message from her, short and sweet. 'Parts arrived in the UK. Job well done. Your cheque is in the post.'

Chapter 11

The heli had transferred the Tac Nuke to a Saudi military base for further evaluation, and on its return flight, it brought a passenger, Anwar, for a consultation with Harper and Laiya. 'Despite one or two small problems,' Anwar said, with a sidelong glance at Harper, 'we are pleased with the results of the first two operations and now, as promised, it is time to turn our attention to the matter of Colonel Channarong. We have a common target and as I said before, I see no reason why we should not pool our resources to our mutual advantage. We can provide any assistance you require with a cover story, surveillance, background intelligence, recces, and armed support, and anything else you need to lure this individual to a place from where we can abduct him without anyone being any the wiser.'

Harper raised an eyebrow. 'You want him alive, then?'

'Indeed. Powerful individuals in the Kingdom wish to confront this person with his crimes and personally mete out the appropriate punishment, but before that can be allowed to happen we need to be certain that there will be no further problems from that quarter. So first he will need to be persuaded to tell us with whom, if anyone, he has shared his knowledge of the matter at hand, and as you know, eliciting such information can sometimes be a lengthy process.' He gave a chilling smile. 'Even with all the specialised facilities we have at our disposal.'

Harper kept his expression neutral. The formalities of Saudi etiquette seemed to require even a one word answer to last for several sentences. 'Understood,' he said.

'There is no possibility of abducting Channarong from Thailand without the risk of a calamitous diplomatic incident if it goes wrong,' said Anwar. 'Nor is he stupid enough to agree to fly to Saudi Arabia, so we need to lure him to a third country, where he will feel secure, but where we can target him and secure him with minimal risk of any PR blow-back. Now, recently he has been demanding regular payments from a wealthy Saudi individual, to protect his sons from a criminal investigation. The amounts paid have been relatively modest - $100,000 each time, but it is most definitely extortion.'

Harper had to hide a smile at the Saudi definition of 'relatively modest'.

'However, despite repeated assurances that there would be no more demands,' Anwar said, 'he keeps asking for more. Therefore, I suggest that we make an approach through the channels he has already been using, saying that our principal is tiring of this and wants to put this irritation behind him once and for all. We will therefore propose to him that we make a single, substantial payment in cash, in dollars, in return for all the surveillance footage, phone tap intercepts etc, that he holds, making an end of the matter. Would you say that one or two million dollars would be enough to achieve our purpose?'

'It would for me,' Harper said, 'but since we're not intending to hand over any money anyway, why not make it five million dollars? That way his greed is more likely to overwhelm any reservations he might have. However, if it's going to work, we'll need a plausible location for the hand-over. How about we use the *Al Shaheen*?'

'Very well,' Anwar said. 'I will overview the conduct of the op from the operations centre on the *Al Shaheen* where I shall station myself. We will also stream the operation live to our Defence Headquarters in Riyadh so our superiors can see what their dollars are buying.'

'Sounds like a plan,' said Harper. 'Now there's a little port called Portofino on Italy's Ligurian coast. It's a real haven of the super rich - like Monaco but a lot less trashy - and there are always a lot of super-yachts, millionaires and billionaires cruising around there in summer. If you can have the *Al Shaheen* sail there, we can not only use it to support the legend we're creating, it will also act as the base for the op. As usual, we will need the ship to arrive with all flags flying and lit up from stem to stern because we must create the impression that the Saudi playboys are coming to Portofino to party. We're also going to need at least a dozen of our team of special ops guys in addition to the crew the ship carries, and we'll require some other logistical support as well: comms kit, weaponry and other supplies, and several vehicles, including a goods van and a couple of heavy lorries.'

They spent several more hours developing and refining the plan, but Harper was confident that it would work, always provided that the Thai colonel took the bait. Within two days he had the answer. Channarong had agreed to fly to Italy, hand over the incriminating documents and film footage he held, and in return collect an enormous cash payment in full and final settlement.

'He won't agree to board the yacht,' Anwar told Harper. 'He said he would only meet us in a public place, like a restaurant, where we can do the handover in full view of his security team.'

'That's fine,' Harper said, 'I never expected he'd agree to go on board, but as long as he's in country and heading for Portofino, we've got him.'

Chapter 12

Once more Harper had called on Hansfree's electronics wizardry and he had little difficulty in hacking into the Thai Airlines' booking system and discovering Channarong's flight plans. 'He's travelling with another Thai, presumably his bodyguard, and they're booked - first class naturally - on a flight into Rome, connecting with a commuter flight to Pisa,' said Hansfree.

'Great work, Hansfree,' Harper said.

'Wait, there's more,' Hansfree said. 'They are then picking up a top of the range Merc.'

'Chauffeur driven or self driven?'

'Self-driven.'

'Excellent, that makes things easier.'

Harper updated the Saudis and their surveillance team flew out to Pisa at once, ready to monitor Channarong's arrival and his progress towards Portofino. Two of the surveillance team then made a covert entry to the rental company's compound under cover of darkness and fixed a tracking device to the Mercedes reserved for Channarong. They also attached a tyre exploding device to the inside of one of the front tyres. It was invisible to anyone walking around the car and only a trained eye would have spotted it even if they had wormed their way under the chassis.

The *Al Shaheen* had already sailed into Portofino. In summertime there were always plenty of super yachts around Portofino but this one was half as big again as the largest of the other yachts there. As soon as it berthed, tenders were shuttling between the yacht and Portofino, Rapallo and other towns up and down the coast, stocking up on vintage champagne, first growth claret and burgundy, and exotic foods. Meanwhile, a cadre of free-spending young Saudis were glad-handing VIPs, chatting up beautiful models and generally creating a buzz about what was already being described as 'the party of the season' to be held on the yacht the following week. It was the talk of every fashionable restaurant on the Ligurian coast and as far away as Florence, Milan and Monte Carlo, with the rich and super-rich falling over themselves to get an invitation.

To Harper's delight, the Saudis also reported that two men who appeared to be of Thai nationality had been sighted around the harbour. They might only have been tourists except that they were paying the Saudi yacht an undue amount of attention and photographing it. Communication intercepts revealed that long-distance calls had been made from a mobile phone in the area to a Thai number linked to Channarong. 'He's taken the bait,' Harper said. 'We're definitely in business.'

Harper had already surveyed the route that the Thais were likely to take to Portofino. The obvious route, the dual carriageway autostrada built in recent years with lavish EU grants, ran from Pisa to within the last few miles to Portofino, but offered no realistic opportunities for an ambush. The old main road though the mountains and along the coast, the *Strada Statale* 1, following the line of the ancient *Via Aurelia* that dated back to Roman times, offered far more opportunities.

It was a twisting, serpentine road running through the coastal ranges and the mountains of the Cinque Terre, with frequent sharp bends, steep climbs and descents. Even the Romans hadn't been able to build straight roads through the terrain. There were long stretches of forest punctuated by bridges over steep ravines, and small, sleepy villages, their shutters closed against the fierce midday sun. The sea was never far away but remained invisible, hidden by trees and steep rocky hillsides.

About twenty miles from Portofino, just before the road descended from the mountains to run all the way along the Ligurian coast to Portofino, a broad but rough gravel track led off the side of the road, just before the crash barriers as the *Strada Statale* 1 crossed a steep, densely wooded ravine. The gravel track curved around, out of sight of the road, to the back of a group of ruinous buildings, all that was left of the stone or marble quarry that had long since fallen into disuse and been abandoned. A rusting chain-link fence still blocked the entrance, though it looked as if a strong gust of wind would have blown it down. The buildings were all roofless, the shattered earthenware roof-tiles piled in heaps inside the crumbling walls and that, as much as its precarious position above the precipitous ravine, had probably led to the erection of a now sun-faded sign reading *Attenzione! Fabbricati Pericolanti!*

The sign may have had some effect, for there were no recent tyre-tracks or footprints in the dusty surface of the gravel track, nor any sign of recent activity. Even the graffiti daubed on the outer wall looked as if it had been there for years. Harper pulled over, stopped the engine and got out. He stood listening for a few moments, hearing nothing but birdsong and the wind in the trees, walked a little way along the track, then glanced back at the road and nodded to the others. This would be the place.

That night the whole team assembled below decks on the *Al Shaheen* to finalise the details of the ambush. 'As well as securing Channarong,' Anwar said, 'we need to dispose of his car and his bodyguard.'

Harper left the Saudis to prepare the ambush point and arrange the necessary diversion for the Thais while he went ashore, drove back to the town where he had hired his car and traded it in for a Fiat Ducato van. He then drove to a shop specialising in the finest quality Persian rugs and carpets, where he bought a large rug, paying cash, and loaded it into the van. He bought some food and water for himself and the Saudis, then returned to the ambush point. He parked the van well out of sight up the gravel track, and they settled down to wait.

The rest of the Saudi surveillance team kept up a stream of updates as Channarong and his bodyguard flew in the next morning, picked up their hired limousine and began the drive to Portofino. The Saudi followers had four cars in front and behind the Thais, rotating their positions so that even if in full counter-surveillance mode, Channarong would have had difficulty in detecting them. Further up the road, two large lorries were parked in a service area, the Saudi drivers awaiting the signal to rejoin the traffic.

As the Thais were speeding up the autostrada, approaching a junction with *Strada Statale* 1, ahead of them a lumbering lorry was overtaking another one, backing up the following traffic. Suddenly it swerved as if a tyre had blown, and hit the other lorry a glancing blow. Both lorries then skewed to an immediate halt, completely blocking both carriageways. As the following traffic ground to a halt amid a traditional deafening Italian chorus of car-horns, the two lorry drivers jumped out and started shouting and gesticulating at each other. Those cars already past the junction had little option other than to wait, although some did start trying to reverse back down the autostrada to the junction, provoking fresh symphonies of horn-blowing, but those cars just short of the junction began to filter off and take the SS1 instead.

The Saudi followers watched and waited as Channarong's bodyguard, in the driving seat of the Merc, fiddled with the limousine's sat nav, then swung the wheel and took the exit, driving off up the slip road onto the SS1. As soon as the Merc had disappeared from sight, the two lorry-drivers jumped back in their cabs, and set off again up the road in line astern, while the released traffic began to roar past them amid a fresh torrent of fist-waving and horn-sounding.

Alerted by a burst transmission on their comms, Harper and the other Saudis took up their positions, hiding in the bushes lining the verge alongside the road. There was no guarantee that other vehicles would not pass through while the ambush was taking place, but even if they did, they would be unlikely to notice anything other than a broken down car at the side of the road. If someone stopped, then action would be needed but Harper was confident he could deal with any likely situation without creating further problems or unnecessary casualties.

The Saudi followers had dropped well back from the Merc on the much quieter road, but were keeping Harper updated on its position using the data from the tracking device. When it was a mile short of their position, Harper called 'Stand by! Stand by!' to the Saudis, who were crouched in the bushes a hundred yards up the road in the direction from which the Thais were coming.

There was a false alarm as a BMW swept past and then the Merc came into view. As it reached their position, the Saudis detonated the tyre exploder, which immediately blew out the front tyre. Just as Harper had planned, the driver fought the wheel of the Merc for a few moments, fish-tailing up the road, but as he caught sight of the gravel track, he pulled off and ground to a halt with the front wheels close to the precipitous drop into the ravine.

Harper remained in cover, watching as Channarong berated the hapless bodyguard. Channarong remained in the back seat of the car, smoking furiously, while the bodyguard got out, looked at the tyre and then opened the boot to search for a spare. He was still bent over, rummaging beneath the carpet in the boot, when Harper crept up behind him and walloped him on the back of the head with a rock. The bodyguard fell without a sound. Harper stepped to the side of the car, and opened the rear door.

Channarong turned towards him, a fresh curse forming on his lips, but his voice died away and his expression turned from fury to terror as he saw not his bodyguard but Harper standing there, with the pistol he was holding pointing straight at Channarong's face. 'Remember me?' said Harper.

Channarong's lips moved but no sound emerged.

Harper checked for traffic noise and, hearing none, motioned Channarong to get out of the car. He made him kneel in the dirt at the side of the track, hidden from sight of the road by the Mercedes. Thinking he was about to be executed, Channarong began begging for his life, promising Harper a million dollars to spare his life, but Harper remained silent, implacable, and the terrified Thai pissed himself in his fright.

The Saudis dragged the bodyguard's body out of sight, then rolled it up in a length of chain link fencing they had cut from the fence around the old quarry and weighted it with lumps of scrap iron and stone.

Meanwhile Harper silenced Channarong by laying him out with a single, vicious blow to the back of the neck, then cable-tied his wrists and ankles, and forced a ball-gag into his mouth. He then took the expensive Persian rug out of the back of the van, opened it out and dragged the unconscious Channarong on to it. As he rolled it up again with the Thai inside it, there was the thunder of rotors and the helicopter from *Al Shaheen* went into a hover and landed alongside him, whipping up a storm of dust, twigs and torn leaves.

As it cleared, Harper and the two Saudis loaded the carpet and the body of the bodyguard into the heli. Harper jumped in behind them and it was airborne again at once, heading for the coast.

One of Harper's Saudi back-up team was already replacing the Mercedes tyre, while the other one threw what was left of the destroyed tyre into the ravine. They then drove the Mercedes and Harper's hired van back to Pisa airport and parked them at the far end of the rental compound. They threw the keys into the bushes and then walked to the terminal and caught a flight to Rome from where they could fly direct back to Riyadh.

When the disappearance of Channarong and his bodyguard were noted, the Thai authorities would be able to track their movements by the records of the airline and car hire company, but they would then hit a brick wall. Lacking any further information, the obvious conclusion, or so Harper hoped, would be that the notoriously corrupt Channarong had finally accumulated enough cash to flee Thailand for a new life under a new identity somewhere else in the world, and had made careful plans to cover his tracks in case of pursuit.

The heli had meanwhile crossed the coast, but instead of making directly for Portofino, the pilot continued out to sea, until the coast and its water-borne traffic was just a faint blur in the haze. It then went into a hover while Harper slid open the cabin door, manhandled the bodyguard's body to the edge and pushed it out. It hit the sea with a splash of foam and green water and sank without trace at once. The weights would keep it pinned to the bottom and the mesh of the chain link would allow fish, crabs and lob-sters to get at the body. Even if it was discovered one day, by then the body would be nothing but bones.

The heli then turned back towards the coast, landing on the deck of the *Al Shaheen* in the harbour at Portofino. Before the rotors had stopped turning, Harper had shouldered the carpet and jumped down from the heli. If anyone had been watching from the shore, they would merely have seen the owner's latest extravagance, a luxurious Persian rug, being lifted out of the helicopter.

Harper made his way below decks to the Ops Centre where the Commander was talking with his counterparts in Riyadh. With the air of a stage magician unveiling his signature trick, Harper unrolled the carpet, sending the now fully conscious and absolutely terrified Colonel Channarong tumbling onto the deck. After hauling him upright and jerking his head back so he was looking straight into the camera that was sending images back to Riyadh, reassuring them that they did indeed have their man, two of the Saudi black ops team took Channarong away at once, locking him in a cell deep in the hull.

'I have just finished speaking to my superiors in Riyadh,' said Anwar. 'They are very, very pleased with the way the operation was carried out. They look forward to entertaining you again in our country in the near future and showing you their gratitude. In the meantime, to maintain the legend we've created and continue the distraction, we have a party to organise, and I think it will be better, my dear Lex, if you sit this one out.'

The Saudis showed him to a sumptuous cabin further below decks where Harper settled back for the evening with a bottle of Krug, a super-Tuscan red wine and some delicious Italian canapés for company. The faint sounds of music and laughter and the noise of the coming and going of the ship's tenders filtering down to him showed him that the party for Portofino's rich and famous was in full swing. By the early hours the sounds were growing fainter and eventually ceased altogether, but by then Harper had drunk most of the champagne and wine, and was fast sleep.

The rumble of the engines woke him the next morning. Venturing out on deck, he climbed into the heli, which took him back ashore, dropping him on a quiet stretch of road a few hundred yards from the town. As he walked down to the harbour to catch the coastal ferry to Rapallo, he caught his last glimpse of the *Al Shaheen* as it dipped below the horizon, far out on the open sea.

About the Author

Stephen Leather is one of the UK's most successful thriller writers, an eBook and *Sunday Times* bestseller and author of the critically acclaimed Dan "Spider" Shepherd series and the Jack Nightingale supernatural detective novels. Before becoming a novelist he was a journalist for more than ten years on newspapers such as *The Times*, the *Daily Mirror*, the *Glasgow Herald*, the *Daily Mail* and the *South China Morning Post* in Hong Kong. He is one of the country's most successful eBook authors and his eBooks have topped the Amazon Kindle charts in the UK and the US. *The Bookseller* magazine named him as one of the 100 most influential people in the UK publishing world.

Born in Manchester, he began writing full-time in 1992. His bestsellers have been translated into fifteen languages. He has also written for television shows such as *London's Burning*, *The Knock* and the BBC's *Murder in Mind* series, Two of his novels, *The Stretch* and *The Bombmaker*, were filmed for TV and

The Chinaman is now a major motion picture starring Pierce Brosnan and Jackie Chan.

To find out more, you can visit his website at www.stephenleather.com.

The Runner

The explosive new stand-alone thriller from the author of the Spider Shepherd series.

Sally Page is an MI5 'footie', a junior Secret Service Agent who maintains 'legends': fake identities or footprints used by real spies. Her day consists of maintaining flats and houses where the legends allegedly live, doing online shopping, using payment, loyalty and travel cards and going on social media in their names - anything to give the impression to hostile surveillance that the legends are living, breathing individuals.

One day she goes out for a coffee run from the safe house from which she and her fellow footies operate. When she comes back they have all been murdered and she barely escapes with her own life. She is on the run: but from whom she has no idea. Worse, her bosses at MI5 seem powerless to help her. To live, she will have to use all the lies and false identities she has so carefully created while discovering the truth …

Hodder and Stoughton have published sixteen books featuring Dan 'Spider' Shepherd written by Sunday Times bestselling author Stephen Leather. His standalone thriller The Runner, featuring characters from the Spider Shepherd books, will be published in January 2020.

28841859R00130

Printed in Great Britain
by Amazon